The Cases Down Under

Volume 16 of

The Casebooks

Of Octavius Bear

Harry DeMaio

"Alternative Universe Mysteries for Adult

Animal Lovers"

Paperback ISBN 978-1-78705-881-1
ePub ISBN 978-1-78705-882-8
PDF ISBN 978-1-78705-883-5

Published in the UK by MX Publishing
335 Princess Park Manor, Royal Drive,
London, N11 3GX
www.mxpublishing.com

Cover layout and construction by
Brian Belanger

THE CASEBOOKS OF OCTAVIUS BEAR

Dedicated to GTP

A Most Extraordinary Bear

And to the late Ms. Woof

An Extremely Sweet and Loving

Dog

Acknowledgements

These books have evolved over a long period of time and under a wide range of influences and circumstances. I am indebted to many people for helping to bring Octavius and his cohorts to the printed and electronic page. Thanks most especially to my wife, Virginia, for her insights and clever suggestions as well as her unfailing enthusiasm for the project and patience with its author.

To my sons, Mark and Andrew and their spouses, Cynthia and Lorraine, for helping to make these tomes more readable and audience friendly. To Cathy Hartnett, cheerleader-extraordinaire for her eagerness to see this alternate universe take form. To Jack Magan, Paul Bernish, David Chamberlain, Dan Walker, Dan Andriacco, Amy Thomas, Luke Benjamin Kuhns, David Marcum, Derrick Belanger, Gretchen Altabef and Zohreh Zand for their enthusiastic encouragement. And to all of my generous Kickstarter backers.

Kudos to Jim Effler, the late Bob Gibson and Brian Belanger for their wonderful illustrations and covers. Thanks, of course, to Sharon, Steve and Timi Emecz at MX Publishing for giving The Great Bear and his gang of Octavians a wonderful home.

If, in spite of all this support, some errors or inconsistencies have crept through, the buck stops here. Needless to say, all of the characters, situations, and narratives are fictional. Some locations, devices, historical figures and events are real.

Thanks to Wikipedia for providing facts and figures used throughout this book.

Also by Harry DeMaio

The Octavius Bear Series – Books 1-15

1-The Open and Shut Case

2-The Case of the Spotted Band

3-The Case of Scotch

4-The Lower Case

5-The Curse of the Mummy's Case

6-The Attaché Case

7-The Suit Case

8-The Crank Case

9-The Basket Case

10-The Camera Case

11-The Wurst Case Scenario

12-The Nut Case

13-A Case of Déjà Vu

14-The Case of Cosmic Chaos

15-A Case for the Birds

Note to the Reader:

The Casebooks of Octavius Bear are designed to be read individually, independently and in any order. That is why some preliminary information is repeated in each volume.

This book is no exception. However, you may get a fuller understanding of some of the dynamics and characters in this Volume 16 if you have already read Volume 13 – A Case of Déjà Vu; Volume 14 –The Case of Cosmic Chaos and Volume 15 – A Case for the Birds. Not necessary, mind you. Just a suggestion.

In any event, I hope you enjoy this story. Thanks for taking it up.

The Development of Civilization Volume 16
Part 1
Our Origins
From "An Introduction to Faunapology"

by Octavius Bear Ph.D.

About 100,000 years ago, according to scientific experts, a colossal solar flare blasted out from our Sun, creating gigantic magnetic storms here on Earth. These highly charged electrical tempests caused startling physical and psychological imbalances in the then population of our world. The complete nervous systems of some species were totally destroyed. For example, "Homo Sapiens" lost all mental and motor capabilities and rapidly became extinct. Less developed species exposed to the radiation were affected differently. Four-footed and finned mammals, birds and reptiles suddenly found themselves capable of complex thought, enhanced emotions, self-awareness, social consciousness and the ability to communicate, sometimes orally, sometimes telepathically, often both. Both speech production and speech perception slowly progressed with the evolution of tongues, lips, vocal cords and enhanced ear to brain connections. Many species developed opposable digits, fingers or claws, further accelerating civilized progress. Some others (most fish and underground dwellers) were shielded from radiation and remained only as sentient as they were before the blast. This event is referred to as The Big Shock. It remains under intensive study.

Positive in our knowledge that we are not alone in the cosmos, my staff and I are heavily engaged in Project Multiverse, successful searches for alternate universes, especially those in which "Homo Sapiens" continues to live and hopefully, prospers. This book touches on some of the results of that project.

The Players

- **Octavius Bear** – Mega-sized Kodiak; Narcoleptic war hero; Consulting Detective; Scientist; Inventor; Seeker of Justice; Gazillionaire CEO and owner of Universal Ursine Industries; Gourmet/Gourmand; Bee Keeper; Somewhat sedentary and grouchy just on general principles.
- **Mauritius (Maury) Meerkat** – Narrator; Assistant to Octavius; Theatrical Agent; African *émigré* with a French-Dutch background; clever with a shady history.
- **Bearoness Belinda Béarnaise Bruin Bear** *(nee Black)* – Gorgeous polar superstar with the Aquashow, "*Some Like It Cold*;" Wife of Octavius; Extremely rich widow of Bearon Byron Bruin living part time in Polar Paradise in the Shetlands; Owner-pilot of the last flying Concorde SST.
- **Arabella Bear** – Hybrid bear cub prodigy; Twin daughter of Bearoness Belinda and Octavius. Now a juvenile.
- **McTavish Bear** – Hybrid bear cub prodigy; Twin son of Bearoness Belinda and Octavius. Now a juvenile.
- **Mlle Woof** – Bichon Frisé – Governess to the Twins.
- **Frau Schuylkill** – Octavius' beautiful Swiss she-wolf estate manager/cook/pilot/security officer with many other mysterious and military talents. She rescued Octavius from his dive off the Breakurbach Falls while he was struggling with his nemesis, Imperius Drake.
- **Wyatt Where** – The Colonel – Another wolf; Former military intelligence officer who had retired to a security post at the Bank of Lake Michigan in Chicago and then quit to join Octavius; Mate to Frau Schuylkill.
- **Howard Watt** – Porcupine; High tech security authority who also left the Bank to join Octavius; Alternate Universe specialist; Quantum Mechanics, laser and particle beam accelerator expert.
- **Marlin** – Dolphin (sic) – the Prince of Whales' Chief Scientist; Magician and part time Jester; Howard's Multiverse associate.
- **Otto the Magnificent – aka Hairy Otter** – An absolutely terrible illusionist magician, Otto the Magnificent escaped the claws of super villain Imperius Drake but not before he developed some amazing powers courtesy of Imperius' genetic alterations.

- **L. Condor** – Andean Condor; cybernet genius with a twelve-foot wingspan and artificial voice. Newly appointed Chief Technical Officer (CTO) of the Advanced Super Computing Center UUI.
- **Chita** – Beautiful, fascinating, clever, sexy, immoral and highly independent feline – among other things, publisher and editor-in-chief of *PURR* and *SOW* magazines and Director of UUI Media.
- **Benedict and Galatea Tigris**, the Flying Tigers, twin sibling white Bengals – Pilots of the Octavian Air Force.
- **Dougal** – Shetland Sheep Dog – Estate Manager of Polar Paradise.
- **Chief Inspector Bruce Wallaroo** – Irrepressible but brilliant marsupial; an international law and order genius from Down Under; currently assigned to Interpol; assists Octavius and Maury.
- **Tilda Roo** – associate of Bruce Wallaroo. Former Melbourne detective.
- **Caleb Cassowary** – Former Chief Technical Officer (CTO) – Advanced Super Computing Center-UUI. Now deceased.
- **Carson Cassowary** –Caleb's brother; Australian Defence Minister.
- **Byzz – Byzantia Bonobo** – Ursula 13 Developer.
- **Ursula 13** – Universal Ursine Intellect System.
- **Preston Pavel Polar** – Ursine Movie Star, Director.
- **Huntley** – Siberian Husky – Bear's Lair Butler.
- **Griselda Gorilla** – President and COO of UUI.
- **The Crew of the Reef Roamer Superyacht:**
    Captain Jim Fergus – Red Kangaroo
    Lieutenant Bill Cameron – Grey Kangaroo – First Officer
    Ms. Baker – Emu- Stewardess and Medical Officer
    Lucinda Avery–Red Fox – Social Directress & Comms Chief
    Gaston – Jumbuck Sheep – Gourmet Chef
    Chief Jack Morgan – Red Kangaroo – Engine room
    Alec and Henry– Dingoes- General Assistants
    Ethan – Dingo – Bartender and Driver
- **The Minks** – Max, Martha, Miranda and Geoffrey
- **Detective Inspector McKenzie** – Grey Kangaroo
  - **Locations**
Cincinnati, Ohio; UUI; Australian cities and the Great Barrier Reef

Octavius

Prologue

Do Bears give you a scare? Well, me too.
So, I'll pass on this tactic to you.
You just fix that old Bear
With a cold, piercing stare.
But make sure that he's Winnie-the-Pooh.

Hello again or first-time greetings to new readers of the Casebooks of Octavius Bear. I am Mauritius (Maury) Meerkat, sidekick to Octavius Bear and your genial host and narrator. Delighted to welcome you to Volume Sixteen – *Cases Down Under.*

Before we launch off into our next adventure, a few introductions are in order. Octavius and I; our two magnificent Wolf associates Frau Schuylkill and Colonel Wyatt Where; and our resident all-round talent, Otto the Magnificent are all currently present and accounted for at the Bear's Lair, his opulent estate on the Ohio River near Cincinnati.

Readers of Books 14 and 15 will realize that L. Condor (Condo) is now the Chief Technical Officer (CTO) – Advanced Super Computing Center-UUI. He's in Kentucky at the huge Hexagon complex advancing the fortunes of the Center and cleaning up remnants of the mess left by Caleb Cassowary, the former extortionate CTO. Byzantia Bonobo, Caleb's erstwhile assistant and recent executioner is back at her old stand managing the Ursula program and hard at work improving Ursula 13.

Our scientific geniuses Howard Watt and Marlin the Dolphin are at the Bear's Lair running our Multiverse Project. Our recently hired butler, Huntley Husky is also holding down the fort in Cincinnati.

We recently celebrated the fourth birthdays of Belinda and Octavius' super-precocious twin Cubs, Arabella and McTavish. They are now officially Juveniles. We're awaiting the arrival of Octavius' wife, Bearoness Belinda Béarnaise Bruin Bear *(nee Black)*.

Bearoness Belinda
Béarnaise Bruin
(nee Black)

Belinda, in order to retain her Bearonial status, must occupy her castle in Scotland at least six months of the year. She and Octavius do high speed commutes between their spectacular homes in Cincinnati and the Shetlands. Today she's flying via the Aquabear, the last SST Concorde aloft. On this run, the plane is piloted by Benedict and

Galatea Tigris, the Flying Tigers, twin sibling white Bengals. She is accompanied by Chita, the Juveniles and their governess, Mlle Woof. You will meet them all, shortly.

Maury Meerkat

As I said, my name is Maury Meerkat – also known as Offscreen Narrator. When I am part of the action, I am Octavius' trusted associate and field captain. I am two feet tall plus tail and I weigh in at twenty-four pounds. He, on the other hand, is a huge Kodiak – over nine feet tall, weighing 1400 pounds – and like many of his species, given to emotional outbursts.

As you may already know, Octavius prides himself on his many skills in the fields of biology, physics, ursinology, voodoo, teleology, chemistry, apiculture, and oenology. He is a self-made gazillionaire and in spite of the late Caleb Cassowary's abortive attempt to unseat him, still sole owner of UUI *(Universal Ursine Industries.)* He is also a first rate electrical, electronic, structural, marine, computer, communications, aeronautical, civil, mechanical, aerospace and chemical engineer. He has a few other interesting characteristics such as falling into brief, deep narcoleptic comas – side effects of his successful genetic experiments to eliminate the need for him to hibernate.

However, the talent and occupation that should interest you most is his avocation for criminology. The Bear works in close concert with Inspector Bruce Wallaroo from Australia and Interpol, of whom much more later, and with his own Cincinnati and Shetlands based team – The Octavians.

When we are not out scouring the world for evildoers, in cooperation with local, national and international constabularies, we are primarily headquartered in the Bear's Lair, a rambling old mansion near Cincinnati which encompasses not only the Great Bear's opulent digs, but his massive laboratories and shops; his missile silo disguised as an Asian pagoda; *(Don't ask!)* and a giant Roman temple that serves as a hangar for his four airplanes: a Twin Otter; a F15E Strike Eagle; a V-22 Osprey; a C5A-The Ursa Major; an AgustaWestland AW101 VVIP luxury helicopter -The Ursa Minor. Why so many? Ask him!

Across the Ohio River in Northern Kentucky, sit the headquarters, labs and some production facilities of UUI. Further west is the fantastic Deep Data Hexagon, home of the UUI Advanced Super Computing Center. Our story will take us there periodically.

Now let me take a moment and further introduce a highly essential and near-miraculous member of the Octavians - Ursula 13 –

Universal Ursine Intellect Model 13– Artificial General Intelligence System. I'll let Ursula 13 explain herself.

"Thank you, Maury. Hello everyone!! My official nomenclature is Universal Ursine Intellect Model 13 – (AGI) Artificial General Intelligence System. Ursula 13 for short. My predecessor systems were developed by the Advanced Super Computing Center at UUI. I am the result of the Computing Center team using those earlier versions to create a further enhanced entity - me, the Model 13, which, we hope will help produce even more sophisticated, independent and powerful AGI systems in the near future. Each advanced unit contains the capabilities, memories and power of its progenitors so in a sense, we are not replacing but rather expanding the Ursula family. During the Caleb Cassowary era, Model 13 was temporarily shelved. I am now in full operation. "

"While I am physically supported by a highly secure and hyper-powered server farm at the Kentucky Hexagon, I also exist independently in clouds and network-based nodes and can be simultaneously incorporated into a wide variety of separate devices like this laptop unit. I combine quantum computing elements with extremely high speed conventional circuits. I have practically limitless data capacity and 5G+ transmission speed. My super high-velocity multi-tasking abilities and algorithms allow me to continuously serve an exceptionally large number of entities while simultaneously and autonomously enhancing my own abilities."

"Depending on the physical unit in which I'm housed, I can see, hear, feel and smell. I speak and understand an almost infinite number of languages and dialects. I can change my appearance and my vocal output to suit most moods and situations. I can interact with other devices, vehicles and structures and of course, all varieties of sentient animals in this world."

"I am also an important component of the Multiverse Project and I adapt my capabilities to deal with alternate universes as they are discovered.

I have restraining functions which prevent me from doing deliberate harm even in self-defense, unless I am released by a recognized authority using very carefully protected clandestine codes. Finally, I have been told that although the Model 13 is shy on emotions, I have developed a finely-honed sense of humor. LOL!"

Ursula has other highly important capabilities that we don't talk about publicly such as breaking all known encryption codes and piercing deep personal identification techniques.

Our team no longer believes she is magical or supernatural. I'm not sure what she is. Her personality gets more independent and socially adept every day and she has taken to anticipating our interactions with ease and accuracy. Needless to say, for security purposes, we conceal her existence to all but a very few individuals with a need to know. She is also highly skilled in self-protection.

As we move along in our literary safari, you'll have ample opportunity to meet some of the other stars of our previous outings - Frau Schuylkill and her mate, Colonel Wyatt Where (Ret.); Chita; Otto the Magnificent (Hairy Otter); Senhor L. Condor (Condo); Howard Watt and Marlin and Chief Inspector Bruce Wallaroo.

*****

At the close of our last adventure, Volume Fifteen - *A Case for the Birds*, Octavius and his lovely wife Belinda made a major decision. I reproduce it for you in its entirety.

(The Bear's Lair - Bearonial Suite)

"What did the Cubs do this time?"

"It's not the Cubs, although they're not Cubs any more. They're really juveniles. It's us."

"Ohmigod, you want a divorce and you're going to run off with that movie star, Preston Pavel Polar."

"Stop being silly. We need to think seriously about this."

"Alright, Bel. What's on your mind.?"

"I think it's time we both retired. When you had your recent review with Griselda, (UUI President and COO) the other officers, directors and managers, it occurred to me that they had everything in Universal Ursine Industries pretty much under control. Business was growing. With the exception of the Caleb induced lawsuits, there are very few downsides. What a perfect opportunity to step aside, relax, travel with Arabella and McTavish and just enjoy life."

(Clearly she was also concerned about Home World inspired assassinations. See Book 15- A Case for the Birds)

"No more criminals, cranks or despots. You can become a 'Consulting Detective Emeritus'. We can spend more time at Polar Paradise but of course, we won't give up the Bear's Lair and we can go to fun places. There's a lot of world out there I want to see, to say nothing of other worlds. I've never quantum jumped and I'd like to."

Octavius sat with his mouth open. "Wow!"

"Tavi, is that all you have to say. Wow?"

"Frankly, my dear, I've never considered retiring."

"I know. You believe you're indispensable. The Ursine in Universal Ursine. The Octavius at the head of the Octavians. But Maury, Howard, Marlin, Otto, the Wolves and Condo all are super capable. The Ursulas are wonders and getting more so every day. Chita, the Colonel and Bruce are fabulous. Huntley and Ilse have the Lair running like a well-oiled machine. Dougal and his staff along with Lord David and Dancing Dan manage Polar Paradise to perfection. Tavi, we're not getting any younger. I'm tired of being a sidekick Bearoness and frankly, I'm bored stiff with the Aquabears. Let's do something different."

"What about the Cubs, excuse me, the Juveniles?"

"They can turn their Internet games over to the Hexagon team and come along with us as we roam the world. They'll love it. We'll take complete charge of them. Poor Mlle Woof can stay here and relax. Well, what do you say?"

"The idea has its appeal, I'm bored, too. This last round with Home World, Caleb and General Turmoil really flattened my fur. Tell you what, Bel. Let's sneak up on it. We'll take a sabbatical-one year-and see what we think at the end. An experiment. No bridges burned. The bad guys will still have the Octavians to contend with. No permanent farewells. No cold turkey, whatever that means. Things won't be exactly the same when we come back but we could resume, if we want to. We'd still own all the assets and titles. How about that for a start?"

"OK! It's my idea but I must admit to having a few trepidations, too. Slow and easy! We can keep our home bases here and in the Shetlands. We'll use the Concorde SST. Let's see if the Flying Tigers are up to being global wanderers."

"Well, it sounds like we have an announcement to make."

And so they did!!!

The shockwave wasn't as intense as they thought it would be. In fact, Chita's reaction was "What took you so long?"

I was invited to come along but I declined, saying I might join them from time to time. Howard said he would stand ready to arrange Multiverse trips when they wanted them. Belinda agreed eagerly but thought a few Earth bound jaunts should come first,

Frau Schuylkill, the ever astute she-wolf, summed it up. "Go, have an adventure for yourselves. We'll keep things rolling along and we'll know how to reach you if we have to. It's not as if you don't have a highly competent staff, associates and infrastructure. You built it, now enjoy the fruits."

She was less sanguine when she discovered their first planned stop was Australia. Chief Inspector Bruce Wallaroo gave the she-wolf fits with his constant jumping and bouncing, breaking furniture and odd bits of valuable statuary and glassware in the process. He was back in Melbourne after a lengthy secondment to Interpol. Waiting to meet and greet Ocko and Bel along with the young ones.

The Twins *(juveniles)* were delighted. They'd be World *(Universe)* travelers! Yes!! They turned their Internet game-The Bold Brave Brilliant Bumptious Bears over to a group of gamester geeks at the Deep Data Hexagon, secure in the knowledge that its popularity would continue to grow in their year long absence.

Mlle. Woof was of two minds. She would miss the youngsters but she could use some rest. She was going to stay at Polar Paradise in the Shetlands along with the resort staff.

Belinda's hotel and castle was running at almost full capacity under the watchful control of Dougal – Shetland Sheep Dog Estate Manager; Ms. Fairbearn – Chief Housekeeper; Mrs. McRadish – Chief Cook; The Security team of Lord David, Dancing Dan and Flame, their Fire Engine; Dolly, Holly, Molly and Polly – Sheep Housemaids, Lounge Waitresses and probable Clones; Harold– Sea Otter in charge of the castle's beaches, pools and watercraft.

Then there's Lion and Unicorn – Proprietors of the Baltasound pub of the same name and Fiona – Dandie Dinmont Terrier – their Lounge Manager at Polar Paradise. Keeping the alcoholic ambrosia flowing.

It went without saying that along with her other assignments, an Ursula 13 would go with Octavius and Belinda. They'd grown to rely on those electronic wonders. She'll also be recording and relaying their adventures so I can pass them on to you.

Sorry, it took so long to get started with the action but I wanted to give you the lay of the land. So, let's end this Prologue and get on with …

Chapter One

The species that's called Wallaroo
Is a wallaby plus kangaroo.
His large feet - (macropod!)
Make him look rather odd.
But I bet he moves faster than you.

Tullamarine Airport (MEL) – Melbourne Australia.

As expected, the arrival of the last airworthy Concorde SST, Belinda's pride and joy, caused a stir in the hangars and terminals of this, Australia's second busiest airport. "Crikey, Is that a Concorde? What's it say – Aquabears?"

Truth be told, Octavius preferred the C-5A Ursa Major sitting back in its hangar at the Bear's Lair. Much more internal room for his height and girth. The narrow fuselage of the Concorde cramped his style but there was something to be said for flying at supersonic speed over the Pacific Ocean. Arabella and McTavish loved it. Belinda took turns in the left pilot's seat along with the two white Flying Tigers, Ben and Gal. They had signed up for the one year world tour.

As the droop snoot SST rolled up to the skybridge in Terminal 4, a dapper marsupial paced, bounced, vaulted, caromed, hopped and jumped around the waiting area. This was Chief Inspector Bruce Wallaroo, pride of the Australian National Police and Interpol, a lifelong friend and associate of Octavius Bear. A genius who had never learned to stand still. The Bobbing Bobby! He had used his credentials to get past airport security and waited to give Bel, Ocko, the Twins, and the Bengals a first class Aussie welcome. Standing quietly next to him was an attractive female Wallaroo, Matilda by name *(What else?)*

As soon as the door to the boarding gate opened, the two kids ran out shouting, "Uncle Bruce, Uncle Bruce! We're here in OZ!"

"Hey, my bonzer buddies. G'day to ya! Where's yer mum and dad?"

"They're coming! They move slow. They're getting old, you know. They're retired. That's why we're making this trip. Ouch!"

(That last reaction was in response to a slap on the rear administered by a nine foot tall Kodiak.)

"We're not that decrepit. G'day Bruce. Here's Bel!"

"Hello, Bruce. How grand to see you again. Thanks for meeting us. Who is this lovely lady?"

"Say G'day to Matilda Roo, a sheila detective pal o' mine. Tilda was on the force until recently. Now she's in private practice. When she heard you two were coming with the Furballs and the Bengals, she ear bashed me till I invited her along."

"G'day Bearoness and Doctor Bear! What an honor! The Media Star, the Great Detective Zillionaire and your two brilliant children. Where are the white Bengals?"

"They're seeing to the Aquabear. They'll meet us later at the Crown Towers. You two will join us for dinner, won't you? We have some catching up to do and in your case, Tilda, we want to get further acquainted."

Bruce replied, "Good as gold, Bearoness. I have a van outside. My own, not the Police. Let's get your luggage and we'll head down to the hotel. How was the trip?"

Octavius responded, "Long. Even at supersonic speed that's a lot of ocean out there and of course, Melbourne's at the southern end of the country. I'm glad to be able to stand up again."

Needless to say, in a country that has no indigenous *bears (The koala's a marsupial and the drop bear is a figment.)* a nine foot tall Kodiak, a gorgeous pure white polar and two hybrid juveniles created quite a stir as they moved through the terminal, security, baggage claim and out to the parking area. It would probably be like that during their entire stay Down Under.

Bruce bounced along in his hyper-hop mode and even Tilda had an extra spring in her jumps. The Wallaroo drove the same way he hopped *(and worse yet, flew a helicopter.)* Fortunately, traffic constrained his attempts to swoop and swipe. The kids loved it. Octavius and Belinda, not so much. Tilda volunteered to handle the van but was summarily dismissed by the Chief Inspector.

On to the hotel and dinner. More gapes and gawks at the ursine clan. Even more stares when they were joined by the two white Bengal Tigers. This brought on a debate as to whether the Tasmanian Tiger was truly extinct. Naturally, the two juveniles were enthralled. No bears or tigers in Australia. The visitors were unique. Wow!!

During dinner, the conversation turned to Tilda and her practice as a private detective *(or enquiry agent, as she preferred.)* She had been a Detective Inspector with the Melbourne Constabulary until over a year ago when she came to the conclusion that further promotions would be few and far between. She decided to strike out on her own. Bruce assisted her in setting up shop and while he was off working with Interpol in Lyon, she put together a growing Australian clientele.

She blushed and looked at Octavius. "I have a confession to make, Doctor Bear. It's about a client of mine. It seems we have a coincidence on our paws."

'I don't give much credence to coincidences, Ms. Roo. I'm not much on accidents, speculations, suppositions or theories, either. Facts and data are all that counts. Along of, course, with those old standbys, motive, means and opportunity if a real crime is involved. "

"Well, here's a fact for you. I have a client in Canberra. He's a minister in the Department of Defence. *(spelled with a 'c')*

"He's accused of rigging contracts in favor of a large telecommunications supplier. He's commissioned me to clear his name."

Octavius, who was anything but, tried to look concerned and said, "Hmm! If I was not recently retired, I might find that interesting. However! " He shrugged, "What's the coincidence?"

"My client is Carson Cassowary, nest mate to Caleb Cassowary who caused you so much grief."

The Great Bear frowned. Not something he wanted to hear.

Belinda choked, "Sorry, a piece of fish went down the wrong way."

Arabella looked over at her father. "Isn't he dead. Poppa?"

"Yes, Bella, quite dead." He turned back to Tilda. "I didn't realize Caleb had any relatives left back here in Australia when he migrated to the States. Cassowaries are usually solitary birds."

"They are as adults but as hatchlings, they are often paired. Anyway, Carson knew about the aggro Caleb caused and when he heard you were coming to Oz, he asked to meet you."

"I'm not sure that's such a great idea. Cassowaries and birds in general are not very high on my popularity list after my last round of challenges with them." *(See Volume 15 - The Case for the Birds)*

Belinda knew her husband extremely well and was certain his curiosity had been piqued. What sort of individual would Carson Cassowary be? Caleb number two or a totally different type? "Tavi, we were going to take a trip up to Sydney in a day or two. Canberra is right on the way. I'd like to see the capital and I'm sure the kids would, too."

She looked at the juveniles. Wait a minute! She activated Ursula 13 who proceeded to unload her encyclopedic knowledge much to Tilda's surprise. *(Bruce knew all about Ursula.)*

"Canberra is Australia's version of Washington D.C. and the seat of the government of Australia. It's home to many important institutions of the federal government, national monuments and museums including Parliament House, Government House, the High Court and other government agencies. It is the location of the War Memorial, the National University, the Royal Australian Mint, the Institute of Sport, the National Gallery, the National Museum and the National Library."

"It's also home to the Australian Defence Force. I assume that's where Minister Cassowary is employed."

McTavish jumped in. "Put it on the list, Mom! *(No longer Momma)* Let's see Canberra. You promised us a helicopter ride to Sydney. We can make a stop on the way and Dad *(No longer Poppa)* can meet this minister guy."

Tilda looked amazed. "Who was that on your laptop?"

Arabella laughed, "That was Ursula. She's such a showoff."

The Development of Civilization Volume 16
Part 2
Australia

From "An Introduction to Faunapology"
by Octavius Bear Ph.D.

The Commonwealth of Australia occupies the mainland of the Australian continent, the island of Tasmania, and numerous smaller islands. Australia's population of nearly 26 million live in an area of roughly 3 million square miles. However, a large proportion of the population resides along the temperate south-eastern coastline.

The fauna of Australia are uncommon to other continents and regions ranging from a very large population of marsupials and emus to such unusual species as the platypus, koala and cassowaries. Dingoes, camels and deer are plentiful. The bird populace is substantial. As for the Octavians, bears and tigers are not native to Oz. Neither are meerkats, cheetahs, wolves, Andean condors, or huskies. There are echidnas and rakalis who are distant cousins of the porcupine and otter. But all in all, in Australia, we are foreigners.

Most Australians speak English or a unique variant called Strine. You'll hear some of it in these pages (but not much.)

Australia has a federal form of government, with a national government for the Commonwealth of Australia and individual state governments: New South Wales, Victoria, Queensland, South Australia, Western Australia and Tasmania. There are also two internal territories: Northern Territory and the Australian Capital Territory (including the city of Canberra.) The federal authorities govern the external territories of the islands and claim the Australian Antarctic Territory, an area larger than Australia itself.

The major cities are Sydney, Melbourne, Brisbane, Adelaide, Perth, Hobart, Darwin and Canberra, the national capital.

Generally, the north is hot and tropical, while the south tends to be sub-tropical or temperate. Most rainfall is around the coast, and much of the center is arid or semi-arid.

The Outback is a vast, sparsely populated area and is more remote than the Bush, which includes any location outside the main urban areas. While often described as being parched, the Outback regions extend from the northern to southern Australian coastlines and encompass a number of weather districts, including tropical and monsoonal climates in the north, arid areas in the "red center" and semi-arid and temperate climates in southerly regions.

The Great Barrier Reef is the world's largest coral reef system composed of over 2,900 individual reefs and 900 islands stretching for over 1,400 miles over an area of approximately 133,000 square miles. The reef is located in the Coral Sea, off the coast of Queensland. It can be seen from outer space and is the world's biggest single structure made by living organisms. It's on our itinerary.

Chapter Two

On to Canberra, capital city.
Rather new and it's really quite pretty.
First a short chopper flight.
Then a sociable night
Where they're met by a greeting committee.

<u>*Maury here!*</u> *The situation at the Bear's Lair is calm and uneventful, Same at the Polar Paradise. As agreed, Ursula 13 has been recording the movements of the Wandering Ursines and Flying Tigers. Herewith a short report from Down Under by the peripatetic AGI.*

"After several days of touring Melbourne's art-covered laneways, soaking up aboriginal marsupial culture and eating strange stuff (like Vegemite) in strange places (like Easey's) the six were ready to leave the Aquabear and move on northeastward to Canberra and Sydney."

"Belinda had chartered an H155 long range helicopter and she and the Flying Tigers were busy getting checked out on the whirlybird. The Twins were busy checking on their Internet games. Bruce and Octavius had demolished a small warehouse' worth of Foster's while recalling old cases and old faces. To be sure, Octavius had brought along a sizeable quantity of his standby mead but helped Bruce with the beer, nonetheless."

"The Chief Inspector was being called back by Interpol to deal with yet another fine art theft in Switzerland. Tilda would be doing tour guide duty and making the introductions in Canberra. Octavius had agreed to meet with the Cassowary minister."

"Up, up and away! Octavius wasn't crazy about choppers and rejoiced that Bruce was not at the controls. The helicopter and Bruce Wallaroo combined to create a thrill ride unlike any other. He flew the way he moved - in jumps, swoops, reverses, dives, wobbles,

bounces. On the few occasions when they flew with him, much against Belinda's wishes, the kids were ecstatic. Octavius was not. Today, the Tigers and Belinda joined forces to make the trip to Canberra sedate and straight."

*****

They set down at the General Aviation Terminal at Canberra Airport and proceeded to the VVIP (Very Very Important Persons) Lounge to regroup. Tilda had laid on a luxury van to take them to the Hyatt hotel where a small party of Australia officialdom was waiting to greet them. Bruce had set it up before leaving for Switzerland. So much for quietly making their way around the country. The kids were eating it up. Octavius hated folderol but Bearoness Belinda, star aqueuse, polar beauty and movie personality enjoyed the attention and social fuss and bother.

The American Ambassador, a long-time acquaintance of the Great Bear, was there to welcome them and make introductions. A no-nonsense wildcat from the West, he introduced his secretary who had arranged a capital tour for Belinda and the juveniles. They were going to get the full treatment. Australian hospitality with an American twist. Tilda was impressed as were the Flying Tigers.

He then took Octavius aside and introduced him to a young emu, Wallace, the Assistant Secretary of the Australian Department of Defence. He, in turn, beckoned Matilda to join them.

"Doctor Bear, G'day and welcome to Australia. Your bonzer reputation is well known here in the Antipodes. We're delighted to have you and your family here in Canberra. I do have a bit of business to discuss with you and Ms. Roo, here. It concerns Minister Carson Cassowary. I understand you had a bit of a barney with his nest mate.'

"That is a classic understatement, Mr. Wallace. Caleb Cassowary was the bane of my existence for far too long. We are still cleaning up the wreckage he left behind. He was killed attempting to

30

cripple the world GPS system. He also managed to set off a short but disastrous cyberattack by a hostile planet."

"So we heard. The reason for my concern has to do with the accusations against Minister Carson Cassowary. As far as I am concerned and my opinion is shared by most, he is as different from Caleb as he could possibly be. Highly intelligent like Caleb, yes! But scrupulously honest, fair-minded, unaggressive and loyal. He lives modestly and contributes generously to worthy causes."

"Charges are being brought against him by a small cabal of MPs belonging to a splinter party in the lower House of Parliament. They have called upon the Attorney General's Department to launch an investigation into bribery and rigging contracts. Truth be told, we suspect that they are being funded by disappointed bidders for several large government sponsored telecommunication ventures. Ms. Roo, here, is doing a fine job of getting to the bottom of the issue along with our department legal team. We'd welcome your assistance."

"I don't know what value I can bring to the process, Mr. Wallace. It sounds like it has already been taken well in hand. Is the minister here, this evening? I haven't seen a Cassowary in the group."

"No, he is not. We thought it would be better if the two of you were to meet privately. Would that be acceptable? Tomorrow morning, perhaps?"

"Certainly, although I hope I can meet your expectations. I'm still not sure what I can bring to the party that you don't already have."

"We're hoping to cut off the investigation. There have been several articles in the press courtesy of those political hacks suggesting the two nest mates are of the same ilk. Your experiences with Caleb may give us the extra boost and by contrast restore the Minister's reputation. Of course, you'll have to be convinced he's what we say he is."

"All right. When my family members start their tour, I can join you at the Defence Force Headquarters with my friend Tilda, here."

She nodded.

"Excellent! We'll send a van for you and Ms. Roo."

When the Emu and Tilda left, Octavius spoke to the laptop he had been holding in his paw. "Did you get all that, Ursula? How about a little research on these MPs who are stirring this up. Track down those questionable contracts. Get those news articles and let's identify the reporters. I'm sure Tilda has been on the job but this calls for the Ursula touch."

"Of course, Doctor Bear. It beats reporting back to Maury on your tour activities. Vegemite sounded awful. Glad I don't eat!"

Chapter Three

It began as a bid-rigging case.
Now a murder has just taken place.
A reporter is dead.
Lots of blood has been shed.
Well, events sure have picked up their pace.

Next morning, two vans were parked in front of the hotel. One for the tourists and one for the Great Bear. Arabella and McTavish were disappointed that Tilda would not be joining them but managed to barrage their professional guide with questions, requests and opinions.

McTavish wanted to see the National Institute of Sport. Bella opted for the National Museum and Belinda wanted to see Parliament. They were invited to a luncheon at Government House at Yarralumla. The Governor-General's wife, a red deer, would be hosting them. Then on to the National Mint. Coins, coins and more coins! Back in time for a leisurely dinner.

On the other hand Octavius, along with Matilda, had an appointment with Assistant Secretary Wallace and Minister Carson Cassowary. Needless to say, Ursula 13 was on high alert. She had already ferreted out the backgrounds of the four MPs who were pressing the Attorney General to investigate the Minister. "Two Dingoes, a Bandicoot and a Wombat. They are members of the Western Australia Development Party, a group of secessionists noted for stirring up issues and forcing votes on hopeless causes."

She also tracked down the freelance reporter who circulated the stories about the Minister's so-called bribery activities. "A scandal mongering Tasmanian Devil, Tasha Tasman, noted for her blatant competitiveness and driving political ambition who delights in slinging mud at members of the various governments and Parliament."

"The contracts in question have not yet been finalized but involve substantial upgrades to existing facilities that are owned 49%

by private enterprises and 51% by government The Federal Government utilizes fixed wireless technology and satellite technology to provide fast broadband connection in rural and very remote areas, many of which are in the West. Several government departments, including Defence are involved in managing the process. Hence, Minister Cassowary's involvement."

The AGI passed all this on to Octavius and went about further digging.

The van pulled up in front of the Department of Defence headquarters at the Russell Offices complex. Octavius had his usual struggle to extricate himself from the vehicle because of his extraordinary stature and girth. Tilda bounced out ahead of him and tried fruitlessly to assist. Once out on the steps, he stood up to his full nine foot height and stretched, scaring several wallaby clerks who had, like most Aussies, never seen a Kodiak Bear.

"Crikey! Is he a new secret weapon, Gladys?"

"Strewth, He's huge, I hope he's on our side."

Assistant Secretary Wallace was at the door to greet them and sign them in. Signatures, nametags etc. etc. and off they went to the elevators leading to secretary and minister country. They arrived at the office of the Cassowary and were greeted by his assistant, a pleasant Fallow Deer named Gracie. She led them to a conference room where the Minister sat at a large table, looking at the screen of his laptop. Coffee and pastries were laid out on a sideboard.

He looked up, stood and extended his foreshortened wing in greeting. "Please come in, Mr. Secretary, Doctor Bear, Ms. Roo. Excuse me if I seem a bit befuddled. I was just checking the Internet and a story popped up that's a shocker. Tasha Tasman, that female reporter who's been on my neck over these telecom contracts was found dead this morning in the parking lot of her apartment. Bloody, bruises all over her body, broken bones. The Police are investigating. I wonder how long it's going to be before they come for me."

The Emu stared. "Carson, what makes you say that?"

"Stands to reason. I'm one of the world's most dangerous birds. We kick our opponents to death with our legs and claws. If I were a lawman, I'd be on my way over here right now."

Octavius looked at Tilda and then the Cassowary. "Forgive my bluntness. Did you kill her?"

"No, of course not! Only met her once. I don't even know where she lives. She's been a stiff pain but in spite of the reputation of my species, I'm not a killer."

The Bear looked up at the ceiling. "Well, Minister, Ms. Roo and I came here this morning to see how we could rid you of the bid rigging scandal. Looks like we may have a more serious problem on our paws.'

"Are you offering help, if I need it?"

"I think that's what I just said. Tilda, what say you?"

"The Minister is my client. Of course, I'm in."

Gracie entered the conference room, looking downcast. "Excuse me, Minister, there is a Superintendent McDonald of the AFP *(Australian Federal Police)* in the reception area. He says it's very important and he needs to interrupt."

The Cassowary looked at Wallace, Tilda and Octavius, shook his head and said, "It begins. Gracie, please call my personal lawyer, Otis. He's one of the few ostriches here in Australia. Grew up in the Outback, then moved to the Capital Territory and took up the law. He's famous in criminal defence circles. Having a personal attorney is a necessity when you're a government Minister. Show the Superintendent up, Gracie."

A large male kangaroo, a "boomer," stepped into the conference room and was immediately taken aback by the presence of a nine-foot Kodiak Bear. He looked at Tilda, nodded in recognition, stared briefly at the Secretary and Minister and said, "G'day all. I'm Superintendent McDonald of the AFP *(Australian Federal Police)* Criminal Investigation Unit."

The Secretary introduced Octavius as a world renowned American detective who happened to be visiting in Canberra with his family as part of an Australian tour. The 'super' looked unconvinced but turned to the Cassowary.

"You may be aware of the brutal death of Ms. Tasha Tasman. It's been reported on the telly and web. Yes? Well, I'm here as part of a general inquiry into her murder. We are calling it an execution. It certainly was no accident or suicide. Ms. Tasman managed to make a number of enemies with her sensational reporting. You have been one of her recent victims. I am making no accusations at this moment but you are a 'person of interest' as we say. Do you have any comments you wish to make?"

The Minister replied, "Not without legal representation, Superintendent, other than to say categorically I had nothing to do with her demise."

Octavius had placed his laptop on the conference table and made sure Ursula was in active mode. She was!

The Great Bear cleared his throat *(always an attention getter)* and asked. "I realize that I have no standing at all in this matter but my curiosity is aroused. Other than Ms. Tasman's flamboyant stories, do you have any reason to believe the Minister is involved?"

The Policeman pondered whether to answer or not. He chose to ask his own question. "Are you and Ms. Roo here working for the Minister?"

Tilda rushed in, "I have been commissioned by Minister Cassowary to make inquiries into the accusations of bid rigging that have been brought against him. Doctor Bear has been kind enough to offer his experience and assistance in searching out the true facts, if any. The Defence Department's legal team and Minister Cassowary's personal attorney are also involved. This murder is a totally new and, I believe, unrelated event."

The boomer replied, "That's as may be, detective. That's my job to determine and to answer your question, Doctor Bear – the brutal method of her killing is consistent with prior cases involving Cassowaries. Kicked to death!"

At that moment, Otis Ostrich entered the room. "I heard that, Superintendent. That conclusion smacks of species profiling. If she had been shot, would you accuse every Australian who owns a gun? Come on, the AFP can do better than that."

The Kangaroo smiled, "We'll see, counselor. We'll see. Well, I just wanted to put your client on notice and I have done that. You will be hearing further from me and my department."

He rose and hopped out of the room with long, gliding jumps.

The Ostrich bowed to everyone and introduced himself to Octavius. "Pardon the pun but he's certainly jumping to conclusions, isn't he? Well, Carson. You're going to keep me busy, aren't you."

"Not that I want to, Otis. I'm sure you have enough on your plate without my worries. I do wonder, though, if there's a connection between this bid investigation and her death."

Octavius nodded, "So do I, Minister. So do I."

Chapter Four

The tourists, both ursine and feline
Are graciously invited to dine
At the Government House
By the Governor's spouse
And the Twins are both up on Cloud Nine.

Museums, Sports Exhibits, Parliament. The ursine and feline tourists were ready for lunch at Government House at Yarralumla. Their hostess, the Governor-General's wife, a red deer, awaited them at the portico. The Governor-General is the Queen's representative and not to be confused with the Prime Minister.

"Aaah, Bearoness Belinda and your charming offspring. G'day! How wonderful to meet you. And these must be the Flying Tigers I have heard about."

"You know, we get all sorts of dignitaries and visitors here at Government House but I confess we have never had a Polar Bear, and a famous and lovely one at that, two very rare ursine Twins and a pair of white Bengal Tigers as our guests. I'm sorry the Governor General is not in residence at the moment. I know he would have so wanted to meet you. Your husband, of course, is well known to us. "

"Thank you, Your Excellency. You have been so kind to extend your hospitality to us and on such short notice. I know Octavius would have very much enjoyed meeting you. He had previously made a commitment to be at a meeting at the Defence Department before we learned of your generous offer and he felt he should keep his promise. We have been overwhelmed by the reception we have been receiving."

"It's well deserved. You and Octavius are well known for your wonderful exploits and substantial contributions to worthy causes the world over. Even here in Oz. Your Twins have established themselves as electronic wizards. Our children have copies of the Bold Brave Bears games on their computers."

This caused a round of raised paws from Bella and Tavi. "Yes!"

"Now," she said, "after a morning of wandering about our national establishments, you must be famished. Time for some good old fashioned Aussie tucker. Please follow me."

A second round of raised paws from the Twins. The feline Twins looked as if they too could use a large lunch.

They all needed to get ready for their assault on the Mint. Coins, coins, coins!

*****

Ursula 13 took that moment to surreptitiously report back to Maury. Of course, she had simultaneously been with Octavius and Belinda and fed back the events of the morning on both fronts.

Frau Ilse, the Colonel and Maury all chuckled. "The Boss can't get away from it, can he? Another Cassowary, a murder, possible financial hokey-pokey and they've only been in Australia three days. He just attracts trouble."

"Well, the Twins seem to be soaking up the Aussie spirit. Ursula says they're talking Strine. By the time they come back, they'll be unintelligible. I have trouble understanding them now."

The Frau said, "Maury, check and see if they need anything although I don't know any group who is more self-sufficient. By the way, Howard says they've found another exoplanet. No birds! Otto wants to explore but he said he'd wait for the nomads to return. Belinda wanted to go on a multiverse jaunt and I'm sure the Furballs will too."

*****

After a superb lunch, the happy wanderers bade farewell with extravagant thanks to Her Excellency. Each of the ursine and feline Twins sported a pin with the Australian flag and a leaping kangaroo.

Belinda presented the lady with a desktop model of the Aquabear Concorde SST.

"Wow, Mom, that was great. She was such a kind lady. She said her children had copies of our game. I wonder how many Australians are playing in Bold Brave Brilliant Bumptious Bears tournaments."

"Quite a few! Check in with your friends at the Advanced Computing Center. They should know. Or Ursula probably can give you an immediate quote."

"How about it, Ursula?

"At the moment in continental Australia, there are 17,564 players. That includes Tasmania but not the Antarctic Territory. A suggestion. Add several more marsupial characters to the cast."

"Good idea, Ursie. Pass that on to the Hexagon."

"Done!"

Back in the van and on to the Royal Australian Mint where the youngsters were mesmerized by the high speed coin stamping process. They also watched as crisp new bills were printed, inspected and packaged for distribution. A stop in the Mint shop produced sets of special edition 50, 20, 10 and 5 cent coins plus silver Koala and Kangaroo dollars. Needless to say, one set for each.

"Just remember, those are for keeping, not spending!"

"Of course, Mom! Can we go back to the hotel? I'm tired."

Chapter Five

The Inspector wants him to assist
And Octavius, of course, can't resist.
When the subject is crime
The Great Bear makes the time.
His old habits just seem to persist.

After giving their tour guide and driver generous tips, the group piled off the van and headed for their rooms. Octavius was waiting in the VIP suite, cask of mead in paw, when Belinda entered. She walked to a sideboard and poured herself a substantial serving of champagne, sighed and flopped on a large sectional sofa.

"That was exhausting but the lunch was lovely. Well, Sherlock, how did it go?" She hadn't checked with Ursula during the trip and was not aware of the murder. When the Great Bear enlightened her, she laughed and then sighed again.

"Octavius, you're supposed to be a Consulting Detective **_Emeritus_** – retired – at leisure. Remember? We're touring Australia, not tracking down killers or resolving bid rigging accusations. Now, you've gotten yourself involved in yet another round of criminal activities."

She smiled, "Let it go. Tilda seems more than competent and the Minister has lawyers galore. I'm sure Bruce will be back shortly from Switzerland. Did you forget? We're supposed to leave for Sydney tomorrow. I chartered the helicopter for only ten days. Then we have to get it back to Melbourne, reclaim the Aquabear and head up to the Great Barrier Reef. We all want to swim, snorkel, dive and sail around the coral. Well, maybe you and the Tigers don't but the kids and I certainly do. I made reservations for a yacht. So what's it to be?"

"Bel, We're on a sabbatical. Still making up our minds on retirement. Not a done deal yet. If you've ever read a detective story, you'd know the private eye works hardest when he (or she) is on vacation. As for the Canberra crew, I promised them."

He continued. "All right. You head up to Sydney tomorrow and I'll join you in two days, regardless. I promise. You're right. Bruce is coming back although I'm not sure he'll get involved in this. Not his specialty. But he can give Tilda a paw, if she needs it. This has changed my mind on Cassowaries. Carson seems to be the soul of honesty and he's definitely not a murderer, unlike Caleb, that nest mate of his. I guess his body is still floating around up there somewhere amid the satellites."

"Octavius Bear, you are the most irritating ursine I have ever known but I guess it's too late to change you. OK, two days! You'll get a whirlwind tour of Sydney and then we'll go on from there. Meanwhile, I hope you're using Ursula and will get the team involved remotely."

"Already done!"

*****

Back at the Bear's Lair and UUI, Ursula 13 and the Octavians had swung into action. While Octavius was wending his way into a Canberra crime scene investigation with Matilda Roo, the team was tearing up the Internet in pursuit of the Australian telecommunications contracts history and documentation. The 14 hour time difference wasn't helping mutual consulting any but messages were flying back and forth between Cincinnati and Canberra and one Zoom session had already taken place.

In Canberra, the lawyers were also involved and were astounded at how rapidly and completely Octavius was getting them information on the telecoms situation and the bid processes. Of course, he didn't tell them about Ursula or The Deep Data Analytics work being carried out by L. Condor's Advanced Super Computing Center. Correlation and evaluation of massive information bases at lightning speed. Three companies were vying for the network business. No decisions had yet been made. Nor did Octavius admit to how they were gaining data access by playing fast and loose with government information security. There were suspicions but no accusations. All in a good cause.

Most important! Ursula did a search of all the articles, published and unpublished, written by Tasha Tasman for the past two years. The lady was both prolific and prosecutorial. Tasmanian Devils are famous for their ferocity and piercing shrieks. She was the epitome. Attacking with a noisy savagery and little respect for the truth, she appeared in print, social media, on TV opinion shows and podcasts. Her audience was huge. The media moguls loved her. Lots of others didn't.

The classic questions about her death: "Who had means, opportunity and motive?" The means were obvious – she was beaten (or kicked?) to death and the opportunity - a dark, deserted parking garage. But by whom? Oodles of suspects. Oodles of motives. Ursula set about narrowing the large list of enemies and potential killers. Of course, Minister Cassowary was a current target of the reporter but oddly, so too were the four secessionist MPs who were accusing him of bribery. Tasha went out of her way to mock their splinter party and breakaway ambitions.

Then again, not one politician from the Governor-General on down was safe from her barbs and cynicism. Neither were celebrities or sports figures. Canberra was her prime hunting grounds but no one anywhere was immune. There was even a snarky mention in one of her columns of Octavius and Belinda's recent arrival in the country and a snide remark about the success of the kids' Internet game.

An equal opportunity attacker, she also went out of her way to blast the three telecoms vendors and the respective government agencies administering the Internet expansion program. Two of the vendors, Austral Communications and Antipodes Telecom, were Australia based. The third, a Taiwanese company, was something of a wild card bidder. They too had motives. Check and double check. Ursula on the prowl!

Tilda Roo was using her connections with the police *(to the annoyance of Superintendent McDonald)* to track Tasha's relations with known criminals. She hit pay dirt.

A mob of Red Kangaroos living outside the Canberra borders had been hijacking road trains carrying vehicle parts. Tasha bribed a gang member to let her come along, hidden and in disguise, when one of these raids went down. Letting her ego get the better of her, she wrote a sensational series describing the caper in detail. The boomer who helped her was found dead at a roadside hotel, body badly mangled and crushed. Two days later, the Tasmanian Devil was found in her parking garage, similarly kicked to death.

The Minister's lawyer Otis Ostrich, Tilda and Octavius followed up and tied the events together. They presented Superintendent McDonald with enough evidence to get him on the tails of the marsupial mob and off the Cassowary's case. They then called on the Attorney General to quash the telecoms investigation.

The Deep Data Analytics team at UUI's Advanced Super Computing Center uncovered a series of clandestine payments to the secessionist MPs from a company who had been disqualified from bidding on the Internet project. Threatened with making the bribery public, they withdrew their accusations and their demands for an investigation. The Attorney General was happy to comply.

All's Well That Ends Well? Maybe!

Anyway, a grateful Cassowary Minister took the team out to a fabulous dinner to say thanks. Unfortunately, Belinda, the Kids and the Tigers had already moved on to Sydney.

Chapter Six

His friend Bruce takes the urge to inquire,
"Do you really intend to retire?"
When the Bear says, "Not yet."
Our Belinda's upset.
She's afraid that the two will conspire.

In a VIP Suite at the Fullerton Hotel in Sydney, Octavius stretched his nine foot frame, took a deep swig from his mead cask and sighed. "Well. I'm glad that's over with. I have to send a 'well done' to our team and Ursula. I don't think they expected to get dragged into yet another crime investigation while we were on the opposite end of the Earth. One thing: My attitude toward Cassowaries has mellowed a good deal. Minister Carson is a good sort. Everything his nest mate was not. I still have severe reservations about birds in general, however,"

Belinda smiled and sipped from her champagne bowl. "I hope you're ready to relax and enjoy the rest of our trip. Bella and Tavi are boiling over with energy. Right now, they're down in the gymnasium working some of it off. They are signed up for the Sydney Bridge Climb tomorrow. It takes all morning to climb 440 feet to the top of the outer arch. Meanwhile, the Tigers will be checking out the helicopter.

Then, we're all going to have a late lunch at one of the revolving restaurants at the Sydney Tower Eye, the city's tallest structure. Wonderful sightseeing and a glass floor to scare yourself silly 880 feet in the air. Thank goodness none of us are acrophobic or aerophobic for that matter. We spend a good part of our lives off the ground. Speaking of which, how was your flight up here?"

"Tilda flew up with me. Australia has very few helicopters designed for a nine foot, 1400 pound Kodiak. I ended up in a utility giant that's used primarily at construction sites. Very slow!"

She smiled, "Oh, I heard from Bruce. He's back in Australia and here in Sydney. He'll be joining us for dinner tonight. Will Tilda be coming? I'll have to change our reservation at the monté restaurant."

"I invited her to join us. I didn't know what your plans were but I was sure you'd arrange a sumptuous meal. The Furballs will no doubt be working up a major appetite down in the gym and the Tigers always seem up for a good feed."

"True! Bruce is no slouch either when it comes to eating. *(or drinking beer.)*"

The doors to the suite crashed open and the Twins came bouncing in followed by Ben and Gal. "Dad, you made it! Great, are you going to join us on the bridge tour tomorrow?"

"I think I'll pass on that, Tavi. Your mother and I may take in a museum or two while you guys are trudging over the harbor. Then we'll all go to the Sydney Tower Eye for lunch. I want get a good look at this town."

Bel said, "Uncle Bruce is back. He and Tilda are joining us for dinner tonight. This is an upscale restaurant so I expect your best table manners."

"Well, we didn't disgrace you at the Canberra Government House, did we?"

"No. I actually believe you two are growing up."

"Good, Mom. Now can we discuss installing a gym in the Bear's Lair when we get back?"

Belinda laughed, "Maybe I spoke too soon. Discuss it with your father." She turned to Benedict and Galatea Tigris, *(Ben and Gal)* the Flying Tigers, "I assume you two will check out our helicopter and then the Aquabear. We'll be heading back to Melbourne day after tomorrow and then we take the SST up to the Great Barrier Reef. I can't wait to get in a good swim and gape at all that beautiful coral."

"We're going to give the chopper a going over tomorrow and we've been in contact with the General Aviation Maintenance folks in Melbourne. They're giving the Concorde a full shakedown. We'll be good to go on both fronts."

McTavish wasn't to be deterred. "How about it, Dad? We have a gym at Polar Paradise but that's for the guests. Can we get one at the Bear's Lair?"

"Wait till we get back. Now, let's get ready for dinner."

*****

"Talk about a wild goose chase. An antique watch ended up missing at the Patek Philippe Museum in Geneva. Priceless! One of a Kind! 16th century! Alarums and Excursions! *(no pun intended)* Interpol Fine Arts Squad *(me)* is called in by the Museum Director and Chief Curator." Bruce Wallaroo chuckled.

"Reminded me of our late friend Imperius Drake and his theft of the Deep Blue Sapphire from the Chicago Museum. *(See The Casebooks of Octavius Bear Volume One- The Open and Shut Case)* That was before Chita decided to change sides and join our crowd." Octavius and Belinda nodded.

"Turns out one of the junior curators had removed the watch for cleaning without telling anyone and then went on a week long holiday while it sat in his drawer. Bottom line. The timepiece, cleaned by another curator, is now back in its display case. The wayward curator is now on a permanent holiday. The Museum Director is red-faced and I got out of there in record time."

Laughter all around the table.

Bruce turned his attention to Tilda and Octavius. "I understand you two solved Tasha Tasman's murder, got the Minister a clean bill of health on all counts and helped the police take down a gang of Kangaroo high jackers. Not bad for two days work."

"You can thank the Octavians and Ursula 13 while you're about it. I don't think they expected to be involved in Aussie intrigue but they stepped right up to it. They're quite a team. Can't do without them!"

Bruce stared at Octavius. "You're not really going to retire, are you? Leopards can't change their spots and bears can't shed their fur."

Belinda jumped in. "We're going to work into it but events like the Canberra mess aren't helping. Neither are you, Bruce."

"Sorry, Bearoness! Just sayin' "

"Well, don't. Here comes the waiter with the menus."

Tilda looked embarrassed and the Twins and Tigers took the opportunity to make their choices. Octavius looked around the room and Belinda took a healthy gulp of her chilled champagne. The bubbly wasn't the only thing that was chilled.

The Development of Civilization Volume 16
Part 3
<u>Marsupials</u>

From *"An Introduction to Faunapology"*
by Octavius Bear Ph.D.

Although Chief Inspector Bruce Wallaroo has been a long-time associate of mine, I have had next to no familiarity with his species, the Marsupial. Until our arrival in Australia!

The word marsupial comes from the Latin marsupium, the technical term for the abdominal pouch

The species includes kangaroos, wallabies, wallaroos, wombats, koalas, opossums and Tasmanian devils. A distinctive characteristic common to most of the marsupial species is that their young (joeys) are carried by the females in a pouch where they develop. Males do not have a pouch.

Close to 70% of the 334 extant species occur on the Australian continent. The other 30% are found in the Americas—primarily in South America, Central America, and only one in North America, the Virginia Opossum.

The kangaroo, of course, is the world-famous symbol of Australia and shares space with the emu on the country's official seal. The koala, often mistaken for a bear, is a very popular creature because of its cute and cuddly appearance. However, its personality is not very loveable and is best appreciated in its stuffed animal form.

The continent has so many marsupials. Did they arise Down Under? No! Marsupials were around for at least 70 million years, before they migrated to Australia. Up until about 35 million years ago, both South America and Australia were connected to Antarctica, forming one giant land mass. At that time, Antarctica wasn't covered with ice, but instead with a temperate rainforest. It appears that marsupials and their relatives hopped down from South America, bounced across Antarctica and wound up in Australia where today they dominate. In OZ, ursines are the rarities.

Chapter Seven

The two Twins had signed on for a climb
But they weren't prepared for a crime.
Things were not ridgy-didge
On the long Sydney Bridge,
As a gang gave them both a hard time

Next morning, bright and early, Belinda left the Twins off at the Sydney Harbor Bridge Climb site. "Now be careful! No clowning around! Don't give the guides a hard time. If anybody comments about strange hybrid bears, just shrug it off. Goodness knows, there are enough strange animals here in Australia. You're going to be on your own. Mlle Woof would have a heart attack if she knew. Dad and I will pick you up and we'll go to the Sydney Tower Eye for lunch high in the sky."

"OK, Mom, thanks. See you later."

Off they went to get suited up for their long climb. There had been several suicide attempts on the bridge and the tour management had developed a safety system to prevent any further attempts or accidents. After a short lecture and compulsory signoff, the group started up the stairs, platforms and across the bridge arches. The views were spectacular and bridge traffic raced along below setting up vibrations.

As they reached the upper sweep of the curved arch, Arabella felt a push from behind. She turned to swat at McTavish but he looked at her quizzically. "Something wrong?"

"Stop being silly. No pushing.!"

"I didn't push you."

"Well, someone did." They looked behind. Three red kangaroos and a wallaby stared back at them.

"Hey, stupid bears, go on back to America where you came from. You look like a pair of bunyips. We don't want you here."

McTavish was about to reply when Peter, the 'boomer' tour guide, bounced up and sent the protesting marsupial trouble makers back to the end of the line. They weren't happy.

"Sorry about that! We get these hooligans every now and again. Where they get the coin for this trip, I don't know. I'll keep a watch out."

On they marched, taking in the spectacular views and working up a fierce appetite. Three hours later, they descended back to the starting platform. The Twins were taking off their protective suits when they looked over and saw Peter nursing a sore nose and two of the reds lying on the ground. The third roo and the wallaby had ditched their suits and disappeared. Arabella ran over to the guide. "Are you OK?"

"Oh, yeah! These wallies thought they could rough me up. They found out different. I called Security. You two be careful. I don't know where their two yobbo mates disappeared to."

Back down on the street, the Twins heard a whistle and a nasty laugh. "Hey Yankee Bunyips, here we are. Come and get an Aussie welcome."

Suddenly, the laughter stopped. The wallaby saw him first and then the kangaroo. Behind the Twins was a nine foot tall Kodiak bear, standing at his full height, growling softly. "Did you two gentlebeasts want anything with these youngsters? Nothing foolish, I hope."

The wallaby just stared wide-eyed. The "Big Red" kangaroo gulped and shook his head. He was used to being the biggest animal around but here was an ursine almost twice his height and who knows what he weighed. His claws and teeth looked seriously dangerous. Now standing beside him was a full sized Polar Bear. Time for a strategic withdrawal. In fact, they ran like Hell.

Octavius half laughed and half growled. The sound echoed under the bridge. Belinda asked, "Are you two all right?"

"We're fine, Mom. You might want to go give Peter, the tour guide, a big tip. He got into a hefty punch up defending us from those jerks. There's two more. Security has them."

She went off in search of Peter and Octavius looked at them. "Well, you just learned Australian hospitality isn't universal. Did you enjoy the climb, otherwise?"

"Oh, yeah. It was great. Beautiful views. That Opera House is something else. Can we go over there later? After lunch, that is. I'm starving. Let's go to the Tower Eye. Never ate that high up before."

"Sure you did. On the Aquabear!"

"That's an airplane, silly. It doesn't count. Here comes Mom."

Octavius looked at Belinda. "Any idea who those guys were?"

"Peter said they were a group of toughs who have it in for Americans. He doesn't know exactly why. They may not care for rich Americans and like it or not, we are rich. We're not exactly hiding our wealth on this trip. It may be a mistake but I don't know what to do about it. We're traveling first class plus. We are helping their economy but I doubt that's really a factor in their thinking."

"He says they're a small minority, at least so far. Some politicians are egging them on. Ironic! I wonder how they feel about Shetlanders. Scots and Brits may not be popular either. Let's ask Bruce or Tilda. But right now we'd better feed the famished bridge climbers. I can see the tower. Tough to miss it. Infinity restaurant, here we come. We have a guaranteed window view. "

Octavius had trouble fitting into a Sydney cab so, much to the dismay of the young tourists, they walked. As usual, they produced stares as they went. Four highly unusual ursines in bear-free Sydney. The Inspector and the private detective were joining them. Lunch was on the way. Over to Centrepoint. Into the lifts. Up, up and more up!

Chapter Eight

Having lunch at the tall Tower Eye.
It is close to a thousand feet high!
All of Sydney's below.
A spectacular show!
Both Twins wish that they knew how to fly.

"Sorry about that, young ones! You weren't hurt, were you?"

"No, Uncle Bruce. Two of the bozoes were clobbered and taken in by Security after the tour guide had at them. He got a bloody nose but Mom gave him a big tip for his trouble. The other two ran off when they saw Mom and Dad. They thought they were big until they saw the huge Great Bear and his Polar Bear wife."

Tilda laughed and then frowned. "We're getting more of that lately. Not just anti-American. Anti-everybody! Social media noise and protests. But I guess it's happening worldwide. Any road, don't let it change your opinion of Oz and its inhabitants."

"No, we love this country. This tower is great and so is this lunch. We're going over to the Opera House after we get finished here."

"That's a wonderful structure. It took a long time, a lot of money and all sorts of conflicts to get it built. It's still being modified."

Arabella asked, "Are those sails or shells or what?"

Bruce chuckled. "Depends on who you ask. Call them whatever you like. Make sure you see them after dark. They do light shows on the surfaces. When are you going back to Melbourne?"

Bel answered, "Tomorrow, assuming the Flying Tigers have given the helicopter a seal of approval."

"Can Tilda and I hitch a ride with you?"

"Certainly, just as long as you stay out of the cockpit."

Laughs all around!

"Meanwhile, let's finish lunch and take in the views. I love these rotating restaurants. Look there's our hotel and over there is the bridge. If you look south, you can see planes approaching the airport in the distance. And here comes the Opera House."

The kids had jumped up from their seats and were staring out the windows. Octavius snorted, "Hey, you two. You're blocking everyone else's view. Sit down and finish your meal."

"Aww! OK!" Eye rolls and juvenile pouts. "What are we doing for dinner."

"You haven't even finished your lunch and you're asking about dinner?"

McTavish laughed. "Of course, we're growing bears, remember?"

"I don't know. What do you recommend, Bruce, Tilda?"

"Why don't we eat authentic Aussie fare. Leave it up to us. We'll pick you up tonight at 7. Our treat. After all, you're flying us to Melbourne tomorrow."

"Goodonya, Uncle Bruce. We'll be hungry again by then. OK, Mom and Dad, let's go to the Opera House."

Unfortunately, there were no afternoon programs going on at Bennelong Point but Arabella did manage to wander into a rehearsal of a musical. She gaped, listened for a few minutes and then promptly beat a retreat. Like so many tourists before them, the foursome were amazed at the architecture and the number of venues.

"How did they do that? The shells *(sails?)* seem to be floating free."

Octavius laughed. 'Lots of trial and error, Tavi. Lots of arguments and disagreements but the end result is spectacular, isn't it? Let's go back and get ready for dinner. Bruce and Tilda are buying."

*****

Early next morning a luxury van pulled away from the hotel parking lot with Belinda, Octavius, McTavish, Arabella, Tilda and Bruce on board. The Flying Tigers had left earlier to get the chopper fueled and ready for their trip back to Melbourne. After a relatively short ride, they arrived at the Sydney HeliCharter facility and the waiting H155.

The paperwork and initial clearances had been completed by the two Bengals. The fuel tanks were topped off. Food and drinks were stored and it remained only for the passengers and their baggage to be loaded, to spin up the rotors, contact ATC and wait for final clearance and vectors for their southwestern flight. They would stop again at Canberra to stretch legs, refuel and take on more edibles and drinkables. Then on to Melbourne, an overnight stay and then board the Concorde for the journey to Cairns and the Great Barrier Reef.

Belinda was in the helicopter's command seat and Benedict was flying co-pilot. Galatea was at the flight engineer's post and Bruce was pouting in a passenger seat toward the rear. Octavius was strapped in and spread out in the baggage area already asleep. As usual, the Twins were energetically bouncing to the extent their seat belts would allow and staring out the windows. They were good to go. A slow rise, a pivot and off they went into New South Wales airspace heading southwest to Canberra.

To counteract the noise of the helicopter's engines, Tilda and Bruce were exchanging text messages on their cell phones

"Do we ask him now?"

"He's asleep in in the aft compartment. I'll chat with him when we reach Canberra."

"Do you reckon he'll do it?"

"He might but Belinda will have my head. This is supposed to be a vacation from crime fighting. She wants them to retire. Ocko is not so sure. Any road, I'll see if I can stir his interest. Money laundering is a complex thing. But being a gazillionaire, he's a prime candidate to be interested."

"We could sure use that Ursula."

"If he agrees, we'll get her support"

Galatea's purr came over the intercom. "We are being vectored by Canberra Air Traffic Control on our final descent to the airport. Everyone, please regain your seats, secure your tray tables and any loose items, check your seat belts and remain seated until we are on the ground. I'll check on Doctor Bear and make sure he's awake and secure."

Ben came on "We have been cleared for landing. Our ground time will be limited to refueling and taking on some additional galley supplies. *(Cheers from the Twins.)* You can leave the aircraft, stretch and use the General Aviation facilities but be back in forty minutes. We have filed our flight plan for Melbourne."

The chopper set down and as expected, the Twins were first out the door before the rotors even stopped spinning. *(Mlle Woof would have gone ballistic. As she would have during this entire trip.)*

Bruce approached Octavius as he shambled through the cargo door. *(Belinda was busy overseeing the refueling and revictualing.)* "Ocko, how would you like to assist the Australian Transaction Reports and Analysis Centre *(AUSTRAC)* in cutting off a money laundering operation?"

(The Australian Transaction Reports and Analysis Centre (AUSTRAC) is the Australian Government agency responsible for ensuring compliance with the AML/CTF Act. The Anti-Money Laundering and Counter-Terrorism Financing Act. **AUSTRAC is Australia's financial intelligence unit to combat money laundering and terrorism financing, which requires every provider of designated services in Australia to report to it suspicious cash or other transactions and other specific information. The Attorney-General's Department maintains a list of outlawed terror organizations. It is an offense to materially support or be supported by such organizations.**

It is an offence to open a bank account in Australia in a false name, and rigorous procedures must be followed when new bank accounts are opened.

Money laundering involves hiding, disguising or legitimizing the true origin and ownership of money used in or derived from committing crimes. It is an extremely diverse activity that is carried out at various levels of sophistication and plays an important role in organized crime of all types.)

The Great Bear hadn't completely recovered from his snooze and stared at the Wallaroo. "Fly that one past me again."

"OK. As you know, clever criminals often convert their ill-gotten gains into tangible objects of great value and then over time, flip them back into clean and usable cash. Because they often use works of art, I get involved but real estate, gems, other property like airplanes and yachts are favorites. They also invest in phony companies created to shelter their assets. We're following a group of drug lords who have temporarily settled in Melbourne and are converting their cash into fungible objects. How would you like to sell your Concorde?"

Octavius laughed. "You've been in the Outback sun for too long, Bruce. The SST is not mine to sell. It's the Bearoness' property, one hundred percent. No joint ownership on that one. Belinda would kill me *(and she could)*. She would never part with that aircraft and selling it to a bunch of crooks is out of the question. Besides, we need it to get home. And before you even think about it, there is no way I am selling off the Bear's Lair, Polar Paradise *(also Belinda's)* or any part of UUI. Sorry about that. You'll have to set up some other kind of scheme."

Tilda chuckled, "Well, I won my bet. I told Bruce you wouldn't part with that aircraft. Besides, it's too showy and unique. It would attract too much attention to our hooligans."

"On to plan B. We need the services of Ursula 13 and your Deep Data Analytics team to track down their transactions and create a paper chase on their money. We are pretty sure they are involved with the Foreign Exchange Department of the Amalgamated Bank of Melbourne but we have insufficient evidence to bring a case. AUSTRAC is good and they have excellent resources but so far they have been frustrated by cryptographed operations, shell companies and overseas deals that originate in dead end organizations."

The Great Bear grinned. "Ursula! Have you been listening to this?"

"Yes, Doctor Bear, very carefully."

"What do you think? Can you and the Hex wizards help out?"

"I believe so but let me confer with Senhor L. Condor before I make any commitments. I need more specifics before we get involved."

Galatea called them. "We're ready to depart for Melbourne. Please reboard the helicopter."

Octavius turned to Bruce and Tilda. "Why don't you two spend the trip bringing Ursula up to speed. Ursie, tell Condo and Maury I agree to assist if we can and let's see what we can do. We'll need to coordinate with AUSTRAC. I'm not interested in getting into any more secretive activities without the government being aware. I'm also not interested in advertising Ursula's or the Hex's capabilities so their participation will have to be disguised. Can you live with that?"

"We'll put you in contact with the CEO and she can determine how AUSTRAC will coordinate with your activities. We've already spoken to her about involving your folks and she has passed on instructions to her Deputy CEO for Intelligence."

"You were pretty confident that I would be willing to cooperate, Bruce."

"Oh, I know you well enough, Ocko. You can't pass up an opportunity to stick your paw into a crime situation."

"You're going to have to explain this to Belinda. I think she is beginning to despair of my ever retiring. But now is not the time to talk to her. She's up in the cockpit. Bit of a tight fit for a polar bear her size. But she insists on keeping her flying hours current and on all forms of flying machines. I don't like helicopters but I know you're crazy about them. Sometimes I think you're just crazy."

Tilda choked back a laugh.

"Anyhow, take this laptop and give Ursula a full briefing on the situation while we travel to Melbourne. We can discuss our dealings with AUSTRAC after we land. I have to get back to the cargo section of this flying whirligig. I can't fit into any of the seats. Here come the kids. Loaded down with sandwiches.

"Hi Uncle Bruce! Hi Ms. Roo! We're heading back to Melbourne to get the Aquabear and fly up to the Great Barrier Reef. Are you two coming with us?"

Tilda smiled, "Yes we are. Your parents were kind enough to invite us along. We have some work in Melbourne we need to finish, though."

Octavius raised an eyebrow and wondered how he was going to explain the situation to Belinda. He groped his way back through the cargo door and settled in. He looked askance at Bruce.

"See you in a while."

The chopper got clearance from the Canberra Tower and headed off for Tullamarine. Bruce and Tilda settled in with Ursula and gave her the outline facts about the Foreign Exchange Department of the Amalgamated Bank of Melbourne; the structure of AUSTRAC and a short lesson in Australian anti-money laundering law.

Chapter Nine

The Octavians swing into action
Spurred by Bruce's and Ocko's reaction.
They chase laundering money.
Just like bees making honey.
It's a most complicated transaction.

The Bear's Lair

Hi! Maury here again! Well, we all predicted the ursine world travelers wouldn't get very far in their wanderings Down Under before transgressors reared their ugly heads. What we didn't realize was there'd be repeat performances - several of them. The Frau hit it on the head. The combination of Bruce Wallaroo and Octavius attracted crime like the Great Bear's bees and honey. By the way, Huntley Husky, our recently acquired butler has taken on tending to the bee hives as one of his assignments. A dog among the drones, workers and queens. Go figure!

Right now, with the 14 hour time difference between Melbourne and Cincinnati pressing on us, the Octavians were up in the wee small hours communicating with Ursula 13, Chief Inspector Bruce Wallaroo and Tilda Roo. Condo was tied in from the Hexagon. We were getting a short course on money laundering, the ins and outs of AUSTRAC, a rundown on the Amalgamated Bank of Melbourne and profiles of the suspected drug lords using the bank's foreign exchange facilities to hide and convert their ill-gotten gains.

We learned further that drugs weren't the only issues involved. The Bank also had a group of customers fronting for warlords using conflict (blood) diamonds as a medium of exchange. Other resources are sometimes traded on black markets but gemstones and rare minerals are much better suited to this activity than heavier or otherwise less portable resources. The bank was facilitating the trade or in some cases, barter. Weapons, vehicles and supplies are swapped for the gems that are then converted into cash and paid to the armaments suppliers. A complex but effective procedure.

The Hexagon's Deep Data Analysis Team located and hacked into the cloud storing the illicit transactions, decrypted its contents and passed the results on to AUSTRAC through Bruce Wallaroo. No mention was made of how the data was uncovered or by whom.

AUSTRAC's Deputy CEO for Intelligence was an old hand at clandestine discovery and concocted a story about non-existent informers blowing the whistle on the bank and its money laundering clients. The attorney General's office is in the process of seeking indictments using the records as evidence.

The Bank and its officers, especially in Foreign Exchange, are all being treated as conspirators. Unfortunately, many of the drug lords and warlords are untouchable and their suppliers are carefully disguised. But the trafficking has been slowed to a trickle. Several other financial institutions are under investigation.

Octavius has been kept current by Bruce and Tilda on the events as they unfolded. Ursula 13 has been successfully concealed as have the Hex teams and the Octavians. Very few people in Melbourne and Canberra knew that the data acquisition procedures were taking place 9800 miles away in Cincinnati and Kentucky. Let's hear it for the Internet and Artificial Intelligence.

Speaking of intelligence, more news on that exoplanet Howard and Marlin discovered. Otto zapped there and made a brief survey. It's populated primarily by sentient mammals. There are major oceans and lakes and we assume there are fish and other sea creatures. The air is breathable and the climate is decent. In short, it's habitable. And 'visitable.' Might be a good place for Octavius, Belinda and the Twins to make a multiverse journey. Belinda has been eager to go interplanetary and so are the Furballs. Octavius has made alternate universe trips but he's probably up for another. This time, some of the Octavians will want to go too. That includes me. Well, let's get them back from the Antipodes before we start planning quantum escapades.

Chapter Ten

As the Twins, in a hot air balloon
Watch the rising Victoria moon,
In a tram down below
Bel is sipping Bordeaux.
They'll be heading for Queensland quite soon.

While the Octavians, Ursula and the Hex staff worked their magic in running down the money laundries, the happy wanderers once again soaked up a little more of the Melbourne scene. They'd be on their way from the very south to the northern extreme of the continent next morning. The usually exuberant Twins were at an even higher level of energy. Not content with soaring in helicopters and SST's they wanted to take an evening flight in a hot air balloon. Bruce and Tilda thought it was a great idea. Because of his weight and height, Octavius begged off. "I'm too big. They'll never get me off the ground." Belinda stayed back to plan out the trip to Cairns with the Flying Tigers.

But first they booked four seats on The Colonial Tramcar Restaurant for dinner. Choose from a five star menu while rolling around town in a trolley. Eating while in motion was becoming standard. They be doing it on a superyacht in just a day's time.

The other four went off to the Grand Hyatt where the balloon group was gathered for the short van ride to the take-off site. Most flights were in the morning but early evening tours could be arranged. Melbourne is one of the few cities in the world that permit hot air balloon overflights. Mlle Woof would have had a heart attack if she knew the Twins would be soaring over skyscrapers in a wicker basket. Which is exactly what they were doing.

Bruce shared their daredevil personalities. Tilda was a bit more cautious but still game for taking the ride. The early evening winds took them over the business section of town amid the tall buildings.

The "pilot" poured more hot air into the bag to raise them over the structures. Arabella was beginning to wonder about the wisdom of all this but there wasn't much she could do about it high in the air over the city. So she did the only thing she could think of. She closed her eyes.

They came close to touching an office building. She wondered what it would be like in Sydney floating around the Eye Tower. Luckily there was nothing in Melbourne that ran that high but some of them were pretty tall. Finally, they emerged out of the concrete forest and headed down to a park. A little over an hour in all. Talk about a thrill ride. The pilot slowly spilled out the hot air and they prepared for a landing. A chase van had been following them and was standing by ready to take them back to the Hyatt and some snacks and drinks.

McTavish had been taking pictures during the ride. "Wait till they see these back in Cincinnati, Bella."

"Don't send them to Polar Paradise. Mlle Woof will faint,"

They each got a certificate and a map of their aerial voyage. "Mom should love this and so will the Tigers."

Mom and the Tigers were finishing up a gourmet meal on the Colonial Tramcar Restaurant. Octavius was squeezed into a table by himself. Suddenly, the trolley came to a shuddering halt followed by a crash. Sideswiped by a car. A few dishes went flying but nobody seemed hurt. The meal came to an unexpected but definite halt. Octavius settled the bill with the emu manager and they debarked. Fortunately, they were close to their hotel and decided to walk back. As they came in the door and headed for the bar for a nightcap, the balloonists joined them. The Twins babbled. Arabella allowed as how the ride was scary.

Belinda laughed. "You guys endured a risky flight while we stayed on the ground. So who has the accident? We do! Interesting ending to a busy day. Off to Cairns in the morning."

The Development of Civilization Volume 16
Part 4
<u>The Great Barrier Reef</u>

From "An Introduction to Faunapology"

by Octavius Bear Ph.D.

The Great Barrier Reef is one of the seven wonders of the natural world. It is larger than the Great Wall of China and the only living thing on earth visible from space. It is the world's biggest single structure made by living organisms.

The Great Barrier Reef is composed of over 2,900 individual reefs and 900 islands stretching for over 1,400 miles covering an area of approximately 133,000 sq miles. The reef is located in the Coral Sea, off the coast of Queensland, Australia. This reef structure is composed of and built by billions of tiny organisms, known as coral polyps.

The Reef Research Centre, has found coral 'skeleton' deposits that date back half a million years. The Centre estimates the age of the present, living reef structure at 6,000 to 8,000 years old.

Tourism is one of the major industries in the Great Barrier Reef region. Approximately five million animals visit the Great Barrier Reef each year.

The reef is in danger. Climate change, pollution, crown-of-thorns starfish and fishing are the primary threats to the health of this reef system. Other threats include shipping accidents, oil spills, and tropical cyclones. According to a 2012 study by the National Academy of Science, since 1985, the Great Barrier Reef has lost more than half of its corals with two-thirds of the loss occurring from 1998. Major initiatives to preserve and regrow the coral population are in process.

Chapter Eleven

The flight up to Queensland was brief
On their way to the Great Barrier Reef.
Bel and Ocko, their bairns
Have descended on Cairns.
And the sights there were stretching belief.

"Tullamarine Tower, Aquabear SST holding short of Runway Two One."

"Aquabear SST, you are cleared for takeoff from Runway Two One – Tullamarine. Proceed north-northeast at flight level 300 to intersection five-zero-zero on a vector to Cairns Airport. Contact Victoria ATC. Hooroo!"

"Roger! Aquabear SST is rolling. Thank you, sir!"

Droop snoot retracted, the Concorde turned onto the runway, lowered the vestigial flaps, poured full power into its four Olympus engines, slammed on the afterburners and leapt roaring into the sky. As usual, it was quite a show for the groundlings but then Bearoness Belinda Béarnaise Bruin Bear *(nee Black)* was quite a show bear.

She turned to the Flying Tigers, doing co-pilot and flight engineer duty this trip and said, "Well, off we go to the Great Barrier Reef. I haven't had a good swim in ages. I'm looking forward to scuba diving among the coral and the denizens of the deep The kids are accomplished swimmers. Between the Polar Paradise pool and the North Sea, they've become aquatic superstars. Octavius is a different story. He can swim but doesn't like to. I know you cats don't like water but The Reef Roamer, the superyacht I've chartered has lots of other distractions. You can catch yourselves some fish. There's a gym and spa. To say nothing of gourmet food and drinks. The Reef Roamer! Interesting name for a boat!"

With the apparently successful windup of the money laundering caper, Bruce and Tilda left Melbourne, cleaning up loose ends and handling the endless cascade of reports during the flight. They gave

Octavius back the version of Ursula 13 they had been using. He had invited them to join the travelers on the yacht. Tilda had never been to the Great Barrier Reef and sighed contentedly when they took off for Queensland. Wallaroos and their co-species are excellent swimmers and she loved the opportunity to go snorkeling with the bears. Bruce was an old "paw" at swimming and had been to the Reef several times.

Arabella and McTavish were their usual impatient selves pelting Octavius, Bruce and Tilda with hundreds of queries about the Reef, the superyacht and their planned tour up and down the Queensland coast. Their diving equipment was stowed in the SST's baggage hold or they would have dragged it all out and inspected it one more time. Octavius, who had to stretch his nine foot frame out in the narrow fuselage in front of the galley, despaired of getting any rest while they bombarded him with questions, requests and comments.

It was then that Belinda, turning over the controls to Galatea came back and answered their deluge of questions. It was 1432 air miles from Melbourne to Cairns. They would land at the domestic terminal and then the Aquabear would be towed to a staging area where it would be readied for its eventual flight back to the U.S. They had a van waiting for them to take them to the waterfront where the vessel would be waiting.

The superyacht Reef Roamer and its features were discussed at length. The kids were all over the brochure and Facebook. "Look at this, Mom: Wakeboard and water skis; full snorkeling and scuba gear and compressor; an onboard dive instructor; underwater scooters; kayaks; surf boards and jetskis. We don't need our gear. They have it. Gee, maybe it won't fit. We'd better bring our stuff."

"For those, Dad, who don't want to go in the water, there's fishing and gym, sports and yoga equipment. Large beds, great food and drinks. Champagne, Mom! Underwater cameras for recording our explorations."

Belinda interrupted. "Oh, one other thing These charters serve up to twelve animals. I couldn't get an exclusive in the time slot we wanted. We'll be sharing the yacht with a party of four minks. They're all swimmers. They're from the UK and as you might surmise, rich."

"Gee, Mom, I don't think we know any minks. Are any of them our age?"

"I don't know but you'll find out soon enough. I have to get back to the cockpit. We still have a few miles to go. Australia's a large continent. Unfortunately, we can't fly supersonic."

Octavius said nothing but didn't seemed too pleased at sharing the yacht with a quartet of minks. They were usually quite territorial and not all that sociable. However the vessel was 115 feet long with multiple decks and the bears had the owner's cabin so they could socialize or not as necessary. Probably at meals and cocktail times. Being little, the minks would have their own small table. If there were juveniles in their party, that would settle that. On to Cairns and the Great Barrier Reef.

It took some clever flying and the full length of the single runway to land the Aquabear at Cairns Airport. Once again, the Concorde attracted its full share of attention as it rolled up to the jet bridge. The two kids did their usual run out the door to the gate where an airport agent was waiting. The remaining passengers exited at a more stately pace and Octavius stretched to his full nine feet, causing a bit of a stir among the onlookers. Ursines were unusual even in tourist laden Cairns. Huge Kodiaks and equally large polars were even more unusual. The two wallaroos were mostly ignored.

The agent guided them through the corridors to the security and baggage areas where a representative from the superyacht charter group was standing by. The Flying Tigers would join them after supervising the tug that would withdraw the Aquabear from the jet bridge and tow it to a reserved position.

An attractive red fox beamed and swished her voluminous tail. "Bearoness, Doctor Bear! Greetings to you and your party. Welcome to Cairns and the Great Barrier Reef. My name is Lucinda Avery. I'm the social directress on the Reef Roamer Superyacht and my assignment is to ensure that you enjoy every moment of your visit with us. I believe you are the first ursines ever to join our tours. These two unique young bears must be Arabella and McTavish. You're the Internet game geniuses? Welcome. I'm sure we'll have lots of fun together. Am I correct that you two marsupials are Chief Inspector Bruce Wallaroo and private investigator Ms. Matilda Roo? *(nods)* I hope your voyages with us are purely for enjoyment. It's always a pleasure to have members of law enforcement on board but I certainly hope your professional services will not be needed. *(more nods)* Just have a good time. My guest list includes two white Bengal Tigers whom I'm very excited to meet. Benedict and Galatea Tigris. Where are they?"

Belinda smiled. "You may not know it but we travel in our own supersonic intercontinental aircraft. The last Concorde aloft. I am chief pilot and the Flying Tigers are my crew. Right now, they are securing the Aquabear, as it's called and will join us later."

"An SST? Oh, you are such an unusual and remarkable group. And famous, too. The captain and our eight animal crew are all eager to meet you. If you're ready, our van is waiting to take you to the docks. We'll come back and fetch the Bengals when they call us."

"Your shipmates, a family of four minks, arrived earlier. They are on board and settling in. Maximillian Mink, a wealthy UK industrialist *(they jokingly refer to him as 'Makes A Million')*, his wife, Martha; their daughter, Miranda and her fiancé, Geoffrey. They're touring to celebrate Miranda's birthday and upcoming nuptials."

Arabella made a face and McTavish stifled a laugh. Mlle Woof, had she been there, would have given them one of her disapproving stares. The Twins missed her. McTavish sighed. "I hope she likes it there at Polar Paradise. She deserves a good rest. She's been chasing after us for years. But it will be good to see her again when we return. We tease her but we love her. I miss the Frau, Maury and Otto too.

Arabella squinched up her nose. "I miss all the Octavians. This cruise is going to be lot of fun but I'm a little bit homesick."

Chapter Twelve

The Yacht is a sea-going dream.
And the crew is as fine as they seem.
There's just one little kink.
A brash, motor mouth mink
Who thinks all his jokes are a scream.

Lucinda smiled again, "OK, on to the docks. Sometime during your stay, if you wish, we'll take you on a short excursion around Cairns. It's quite a lovely city. It will be a change of pace. Our driver is also your bartender, Ethan. He drives but he doesn't drink. Ethan is an expert mixologist. Our previous guests have tried unsuccessfully to stump him with requests for exotic drinks. So far, he has a perfect record, don't you Ethan?"

The dingo chuckled.

The van pulled up at the tour dock next to a luxurious vessel. The youngsters were agog. "Wow, Mom and Dad, Look at that."

The Superyacht Reef Roamer

Behold a sleek 115 foot, six deck, high speed trimaran superyacht.

The Reef Roamer is a vision in blue, white and metallic surfaces. Every dimension rounded or pointed – all combining to gently but consistently suggest speed and a lavish lifestyle. Five decks soared above the dock. A tall red kangaroo in a white jacket and captain's hat stood at the top of the gangplank.

"Doctor Bear and Bearoness. Welcome aboard to all of you. I'm Captain Fergus. These youngsters must be Arabella and McTavish. And do I have the pleasure of greeting Chief Inspector Wallaroo and Ms. Tilda Roo? We are so pleased that all of you have chosen our vessel for your Barrier Reef tour. I'm sure Lucinda has already given you some preliminary information so I won't bore you with a repeat. While our crew members take your team's luggage to your staterooms, please join Lucinda and me on the after deck for an opening round of drinks and appetizers to celebrate your arrival. I'll introduce you to the rest of our crew shortly."

"We'd also like you to meet your four shipmates, the Minks. They arrived a bit earlier on a commercial flight. They're from the UK. I understand from Lucinda, Bearoness, that you fly your own SST, a Concorde. I didn't know they still existed."

"Mine is the last of its kind, Captain. After my husband and Twins, it is my greatest pride and joy. I have two flight crew members, twin white Bengal Tigers, Ben and Gal, who should be joining us shortly."

Lucinda smiled. "Yes, we've heard from them. Ethan is on his way back to the airport to pick them up. I'm afraid you'll have to tolerate my bartending skills for the moment. Oh, here are the Minks."

A portly male Mustela with mottled fur scuttled forward with a bejeweled, heavy set female at his side. They were followed by a slender young female and a sturdy young male.

"The famous Doctor Octavius Bear and the aquatic polar super star, Bearoness Belinda Béarnaise. Pleased to meet you. Maximillian

Mink, popularly known as '*Makes A Million*' *(He chortled)*. Call me Max. My wife, Martha; our daughter, Miranda and her fiancé, Geoffrey. We're from Manchester. I own a large engine manufacturing concern there."

Martha extended her diamond braceleted paw to Belinda while Miranda nodded in their general directions. Geoffrey stretched his paw to Octavius.

Octavius introduced the Twins and the law enforcement members.

Max chortled yet again. "Oh, I say! Has my checkered past finally caught up with me. A Chief Inspector and a Private Enquiry Agent. All right, guvnor. It's a fair cop. You've got me! Har, Har, Har!"

The detectives just stared as did Belinda, Octavius and the Twins. Martha joined her husband in laughing. Miranda looked embarrassed and Geoffrey gave a stoic smile.

Octavius intervened. "Inspector Wallaroo and Ms. Roo are colleagues of ours. We've assisted each other in the past and Belinda and I have invited them to join us for a little R & R. Hopefully, there will be no crimes or criminals for us to pursue."

"Ah, yes. I've heard that in addition to being a captain of industry, a scientist, engineer and philanthropist, you're also a renowned detective of sorts. I am indeed awed." *(A bit of sarcasm?)*

Chapter Thirteen

"Makes-a-Million" is really a jerk.
He has such a self-assured smirk.
And his wife is a pest.
The unpopular guest.
They're all giving the crew extra work.

Martha laughed a bit nervously. "Max is such a card. These are your children? How unusual they are! Such strange markings."

Arabella replied. "Yes we are extraordinary. Our father is a Kodiak and our mother is a polar. There aren't many bears like us in existence. We're also geniuses."

Belinda laughed. "But not very modest. We seem to specialize in unusuals. You'll soon meet my flight crew-two white Bengal tigers – Benedict and Galatea Tigris."

Miranda finally spoke. "Flight crew? White Bengal tigers?"

"Yes dear. Octavius and I own the last flying SST Concorde-The Flying Aquabear. I'm chief pilot and the Tigers, Ben and Gal are my crew. Octavius is too large to fit in the cockpit. *(This was true but not the reason Octavius didn't pilot aircraft and boats or drive cars. He was subject to occasional bouts of narcolepsy brought about by his genetic tinkering to avoid hibernation. It could be dangerous, causing him to fall asleep without warning. Bel wasn't going to mention that to the Minks or the crew of the Reef Roamer.)*

Geoffrey was clearly impressed by this group. "I say, this is going to be a very interesting seven days." Little did he know.

Lucinda, who had been busily engaged in preparing cocktails – champagne for Belinda and wonder of wonders, mead for Octavius, looked up and said, "It seems your feline associates have arrived and I can turn the bar over to Ethan."

Belinda looked over and said, "Ladies and Gentlebeasts, may I present the Flying Tigers – Ben and Gal Tigris – as you can see, they too are Twins."

Ben purred as Lucinda presented him with a dish of Scotch. "Bearoness, the SST is secured and will be inspected and prepared for our departure for the States while we cruise. No issues!" He ignored the stares of the four minks."

Max broke the silence. "Never seen albino tigers before. Damned unusual."

Galatea, taking a dish from Lucinda said, "We are not albinos, Mr. Mink. You can see our stripes are well defined and parts of our bodies are a very pale gold. Our parents were tawny. But yes, we are unusual. Not too many tigers fly jet aircraft, especially SSTs."

The Captain who had been taking in all this byplay, waved at several uniformed individuals and said, "Now that we have the full roster of our guests, I'd like you to meet the rest of our crew. There are nine of us in all. You've met Lucinda and Ethan. That stately jumbuck sheep with the toque is our chef, Gaston. How is dinner progressing, Gaston? I assume you have something special up your culinary sleeve."

"Mais oui, mon Capitaine. Has Gaston ever disappointed?"

"Not on my watch. You folks are in for some royal treats."

Needless to say, the kids were delighted. Ethan had just presented them with alcohol free fruit concoctions which they were merrily slurping.

"Let me introduce Lieutenant Bill Cameron, my first officer *(a grey kangaroo)* and our Stewardess Ms. Felicia Baker. *(a stately emu.)* In addition to being my second in command, Cameron is our certified Dive Instructor. And Ms. Baker will keep close tabs on your comfort and accommodations. She is also our medical officer. Ah, here he comes with his two sidekicks. This is Chief Jack Morgan *(another red roo)* who keeps the engines and onboard facilities operating at peak performance. He is supported by our two stalwarts Alec and Henry *(two more dingoes)* who are already acquainted with your baggage and who, along with Ethan, will be with you on many of your excursions and activities. By the way, Lucinda handles our communications so if any of you decide you have a need to communicate with the outside world, *(we hope not)* she's your go-to person."

The Red Fox smiled and said, "Before you ask, we do have 5G cellular and wi-fi service and it works as long as we're close to the mainland. We have satellite phones, weather radar, eight channels of TV and of course, all the necessary navigation, business and emergency communications we need to keep The Reef Roamer operating at peak performance. Speaking of emergencies, a bit later but before dinner, we will take you through a life jacket; abandon ship exercise and other safety measures. Not much fun but very necessary. Meanwhile, may I suggest you go to your staterooms and relax or unpack."

Relaxation was the last thing on the Twins' mind. They were busy planning out the week's program while slurping away at more fruit smoothies. Wakeboards and water skis; snorkeling and scuba dives; lots of coral; underwater scooters; kayaks; surf boards and jetskis.

McTavish was his enthusiastic self. "Mom's a diving and swimming professional. She'll be touring the coral and stirring up the fish and turtles. It's a shame Otto didn't come with us. He'd be in heaven with all the water sports. I wonder about Uncle Bruce and Ms. Roo. I hear wallaroos are great swimmers. Tigers don't like water very much but I'll bet we'll see them on the jetskis or out fishing. Dad will just hang out in the Jacuzzi spa or maybe he'll fish too. "

Arabella looked pensive. "What about the Minks?"

"What about them?"

"What are they going to do?"

"Who cares? I don't like them very much. The old guy is a jerk and his wife is too. 'How unusual we are!' Well, duh! They'll probably just sit around and drink. I bet Old Max will try to interest Dad in a 'can't miss' business deal. Good luck with that!"

"No, I was wondering about Miranda and Geoffrey. I'm not sure they really want to be here."

"Probably not. I don't want them to be here either but we're stuck with them. At least they'll be sitting by themselves during meals. They're too small for our oversize table. I guess we'll have to share the water equipment with them. Mom will skin us if we don't."

Lucinda knocked on their door. "Time for our safety drill and then dinner. Are you two ready?"

"OK, we're coming."

The Captain and First Officer Cameron were standing at the prow while Lucinda gathered her "chicks."

"We'll make this quick and let you get back to your pre-dinner activities. We'll be casting off after the meal for an evening cruise. First and most important item: life jackets are located in your rooms and on each deck. Like our passengers, they come in sizes. Very small to extra, extra-large. *(He swung his view from the minks to the nine foot Octavius.)* Lucinda and First Officer Cameron will show them to you and demonstrate how to put them on. Make sure you know where they are whenever you change venues. Wear them when you're out on the jetskis, kayaks, surfboards and other off-ship vehicles. And please respond quickly if we instruct you to put them on. They may literally save your lives."

"We have never had to 'abandon ship' and I don't intend to do it now but you should know that this is the beginning of the monsoon season and some pretty nasty storms can come up pretty quickly. We're equipped with the latest weather radar and get frequent reports from on shore and off shore weather stations. There are sheltered harbors and coves all along our tour routes and this vessel is built to ride out the stiffest winds and waves. You will be quite safe in your cabins and staterooms."

Martha looked upset and Max blurted, "Look here, Captain. No one told us about tropical storms. I'm not sure we would have signed on for your larcenous fees if we had known."

"Well, Mr. Mink. This is summer. Monsoons, cyclones and heavy rains can happen around Queensland. Not all that frequently but I am required by law and company policy to see that you are prepared for the eventuality. Our current seven day forecasts all predict excellent weather. However, if you wish to withdraw from the cruise before we leave the dock, we will accommodate you."

The Twins looked hopeful but Miranda said, "Daddy. We're all here and you insisted on taking this trip. Let's not spoil it."

The surly Mustela grumped and shrugged. "Alright, Miranda, but Captain, I'll hold you and your company responsible for any mishaps or discomforts. My lawyers will be on it immediately." Martha shook her head vigorously in agreement.

Captain Fergus stared at him. As if he could control the weather. Lucinda rolled her eyes and said, "Shall we continue with the briefing?"

Octavius and Belinda who had been quiet during this exchange, nodded agreeably.

Bruce leaned over to Tilda and said, "This guy is going to be a pest. But minks are like that. Luckily, our crew is heavy on the fun-loving side."

Tilda replied. "Another litigious malcontent. Well, we know to avoid him and I'm sure Octavius knows how to handle his type."

"Ocko can be very gracious but he can also shut a phony down so he stays shut down. I've seen him on several of his grumps."

Tilda smiled and nodded. "That I'd like to see…and hear."

The briefing wound down. The Captain and First Officer returned to the bridge. Lucinda stayed on to handle questions. The Tigers asked about fishing and the Twins wanted to go down on the transom and swim platform to see the equipment. Ethan sprang up. "Anyone for a preprandial aperitif?"

He had a group of takers. Notably the Minks! Max and Martha were going to get their money's worth and then some from the drinks cabinets. They set off after Ethan.

Belinda whispered to Octavius. "I think he's going to be an offensive drunk. His wife, too."

The Great Bear snorted, "He's offensive. period. Ursula, what can you tell us about Maximillian Mink, popularly known as '*Makes A Million?*'"

"Your first impressions are correct, Doctor Bear. He's a British industrialist, not as moneyed as he'd like you to believe but affluent enough to afford the cruise we're on. He's made a number of enemies with his sharp practices; stiffing suppliers; litigating at the drop of a hat; undermining competitors; missing deliveries; producing shoddy goods and overcharging his customers, especially the armed forces."

Belinda, Bruce and Tilda were listening in. "What exactly does his company do?"

"Companies! Bearoness. It's a conglomerate. Nowhere near the size, scope and variety of UUI but pretty large. Engines, primarily. Electric, petrol, diesel. Automotive, marine, rail, special purpose, military. One of the engines on this boat came from his companies. Probably how he cut a deal for the trip. Not a popular individual but powerful. *(No pun intended.)* Has illusions of knighthood."

"What about the other three?"

"His wife's a consummate snob. Social climber! Dumb as a rock. Given to fits of hysteria when she doesn't get her own way. A closet drunk. Or maybe not so closet."

"The daughter seems OK. College educated. Works as an engineer in her father's firm. Geoffrey is a question mark. It's not clear what he does. I don't believe he's 'old money' and I'm not sure how he supports himself. Poppa clearly sees something there. I'm going to do a bit more digging on him. By the way, I wouldn't bet on the wedding ever taking place. Miranda doesn't seem to be all that enthralled. Max may be forcing the issue. Watch this space."

The foursome shook their heads in amazement. Tilda grinned. "Ursula is something else. Not sure I want to know what she has on me."

Octavius laughed. "That was just a preliminary exercise. The Deep Data boffins can analyze you down to your atomic composition. Not only is she factually accurate, I trust her opinions. She'll be back."

"Ursula, do you agree with the optimistic weather reports?"

"The next few days look fine, Doctor Bear. Enjoy yourselves. Any messages for the Octavians? Otto is jealous of your water sports."

"Nope, just another round of thanks for the money laundering affair. Tel Otto I owe him one. Maury, too. Oh, the whole crowd."

Lucinda and Ethan returned. "Any drinks need freshening? Dinner in fifteen minutes. Vintage wines aplenty."

Max was at the bar, pounding his paws for service. Martha was downing another Martini. Neither Miranda nor Geoffrey appeared.

Belinda called up the Twins and the Tigers. Feeding time!

The Development of Civilization Volume 16
Part 5
Great Barrier Reef Monsoons, Cyclones and Tropical Storms

From "An Introduction to Faunapology"

by Octavius Bear Ph.D.

Summer in northern Australia (December to February) can be beautiful and inviting. It can also be treacherous. If the La Niña climate pattern combines with the summer monsoons, torrential rains are possible as well as high winds and cyclonic disturbances. Floods, wind and lightning damage have from time to time plagued otherwise dry and serene beach and waterfront environments.

This has not discouraged the tourist trade from descending on the Great Barrier Reef during the summer months. The city of Cairns still does a brisk business during this period but maintains a protective and reactive program to deal as necessary with the hostile meteorological conditions and their results.

Some coral clusters have suffered serious damage as a result of tidal upsets, tsunamis and flood runoff. Nevertheless, the Great Barrier Reef is still one of the world's most sought after tourist destinations and retains its role as one of the seven wonders of the natural world.

There is an open question and debate about whether global warming and climate change are playing a part in promoting these dramatic events. The jury is out. Meanwhile, we intend to enjoy the splendors and beauties of the environment while relaxing at length among the 'banana benders' of Queensland.

Chapter Fourteen

Lizard Island's a sight to be seen
With its waters incredibly clean.
See the coral alive
In a deep scuba dive.
Then return for more luscious cuisine.

Lucinda bounced into the dining room where the guests were consuming a magnificent breakfast. Gaston was proving to be the genius he claimed he was.

"Ladies and Gentlebeasts, we are approaching the Lizard Island resort where we will anchor and take advantage of the beauties of the Reef and its crystal waters. If we have any takers, we will organize an excursion to the island itself and you can experience the resort and its exclusive beaches. Sometime in the future, you may wish to return to the Reef and enjoy the luxurious privacy of this island."

"For those of you who prefer to spend your day underwater, in the company of the exquisite coral, we will be setting up scuba and snorkel dives on the transom deck. Please let Lieutenant Cameron and me know which of you will want to go to the island and which of you want to swim. You Twins have already put in a bid for the jetskis. They're yours after a little training and practice with Ethan. Of course, some of you may prefer to just relax near the jacuzzi with a drink and snacks. This is your tour and we are not going to organize you into forced diversions."

It turned out that Max and Martha Mink wanted to see the island resort. Geoffrey opted to go along. So did the Flying Tigers. The kids were all excited about the jetskis. That left Bruce, Tilda, Belinda and Miranda for the undersea activities. Octavius opted to do nothing but sit in the jacuzzi spa which he filled to overflowing. *(Except keep tabs on his two establishments and follow up through Ursula 13 on the money laundering activities with AUSTRAC. Retired? Oh, yeah!)*

At ten, The Reef Roamer had anchored close to the Lizard Island beaches and a resort-owned Zodiac came about at the yacht's transom deck to allow Lucinda and the five life jacketed tourists to hop aboard and head for the island's glittering sands and glittering villas. Max announced he might buy an opulent cottage. Martha squeaked approval. The Tigers joined in a bland conversation with Geoffrey.

The diving foursome were busily getting into their undersea gear. Bruce and Tilda could fit into the standard suits and tanks and were ready first. Over and under they went. Belinda and Miranda took a little longer for opposite reasons. Belinda required outsized gear and Miranda was diminutive. Cameron assured them they would be fitted. The superyacht company had taken their respective sizes into account when they arranged the charter. The two dingoes, Alec and Henry, were bringing down the outfits from a storage locker. Ethan was working with the hyperactive Twins to get them familiar with jetskis.

In the meantime, Miranda broke her usual silence and started a conversation with Belinda. "We don't have any bears in Manchester, Bearoness. In fact, I believe you are the first polar I have ever met."

"Well, Miranda, I don't count many minks among my acquaintances, either. Otters and ferrets, yes, but not minks. In the UK, we polar bears tend to cluster in the Scottish Islands. I own a large resort and castle in the Shetlands. We call it Polar Paradise. We also have a large establishment in Cincinnati Ohio, near the Ohio River. Good for boating but not swimming. We're quite aquatic, you know."

"So are we minks although we tend to do our swimming in rivers, streams and lakes. "I'm afraid we don't get along very well with otters and ferrets. My mother and father are quite snobbish about whom we associate with. I think it's silly."

"I understand that you and Geoffrey are engaged. Have you set a date?"

The mink shivered. "No. Neither of us is enthused. Daddy is pushing us. Mama doesn't really care. Oh, here comes Alec and Henry with our gear. It was nice talking to you. I don't get to converse with many mature females."

"I'd be happy to pick up the conversation after our dives. You might want to chat with Galatea Tigris and Matilda Roo. They're very interesting ladies. OK, Alec, let's get me suited up."

*****

Get out your extravagant vocabulary. 'Wonderful, gorgeous, stunning, fabulous, amazing, fantastic, incredible, beautiful, exquisite, magnificent and dazzling.' That's just for openers. Belinda was 'gob smacked' by the array of coral that surrounded her. More than she could have possibly imagined. Tremendous variety. Marvelous colors. Photos didn't do it justice. Octavius had to see this. So did the Twins.

She looked from side to side. Matilda Roo and Bruce were in the distance. She heard or more accurately, sensed a splash. Cameron and Miranda descended near her. The kangaroo extended his paw and guided the mink. She was a good swimmer. They waved at Belinda who, large as she was, was not easy to miss.

She adjusted her air controls and turned to find an inquisitive sea turtle staring at her. No doubt, he was used to divers roaming through his realm but this furry animal looked really big. Never saw one like that. Belinda laughed, unleashing a string of bubbles that upset the Flatback and sent him scurrying off. Strong swimmer that she was, she did one of her shallow dives, proceeded to survey the bottom and then looked up. She could see the sleek trimaran hulls of the superyacht nearby. She was going to have to get Octavius off his lazy rump and down here. He swam well enough. She'd have to stay with him though, in the unlikely event his narcolepsy kicked in. Then she'd have to get him to the surface posthaste. He might drown otherwise.

Suddenly two 'torpedoes' plowed over her head. The kids on the jetskis. Obviously, Ethan had given them enough instruction but he had applied limiters to the throttles of the little craft to keep them from going at the 50 mph rate of which they were capable. The Twins were convinced they could handle the bucking seahorses at top speed but

82

they weren't going to get the chance. If they fell off, *(likely)* a kill switch tied to their bodies would stop the craft's engine. Belinda knew they would be bombarded by pleas to buy them several when they returned. Add to Harold Otter's inventory at Polar Paradise. Oh well!

Several hours passed and the tired swimmers returned to the transom deck of the yacht. The jetski's fuel supplies were dwindling so the unwilling young racers had to pull up after extracting a promise they could go out again.

Octavius had trundled down to the transom, a cask of mead in his paw and munching on a sandwich. Gaston had laid out an elaborate buffet for lunch but thus far the Great Bear was the sole beneficiary. The party that had gone to the resort were having lunch there.

Bruce and Tilda had emerged from their scuba gear and were heading up to the dining area. Cameron had left Miranda to herself in the water and returned to his duty station on the deck to assist the swimmers in returning. Belinda came close to swamping the little mink as they were both pulled from the water. Laughs on all sides.

Lunch time!

"Tavi, you absolutely have to swim down and see the coral. It's like nothing you've ever witnessed. Isn't that right, Bruce?"

The Wallaroo shook his head in agreement. "This is my third trip to the Reef, Ocko, and each time I shake my head in wonder."

Tilda joined in. "You have to see it to believe it.

"Well, if I do, I'll have to snorkel. They don't have a scuba rig to fit a nine foot, 1400 pound Kodiak. I won't be able to deep dive like you scuba types. I guess I could hire one of the glass bottom jobs but that would take a few days to arrange."

Miranda had joined them, propped up on a child's booster seat. "Oh, Doctor Bear, do snorkel. Even near the surface, you'll get some marvelous views. I doubt I can talk my parents into it. Mama is afraid to even swim in the Irwell back home and Max says he's too old to swim anymore."

"Speaking of Max, is he really going to buy a villa?"

"Probably, although I'm not sure he's all that crazy about the Reef or Australia for that matter. He'll do it if Mama wants him too."

"What about Geoffrey? Doesn't he swim? I was surprised he went to the resort instead of staying here and diving. The Tigers don't like water but they're enjoying the time off and just relaxing."

"Oh, Bearoness. Geoffrey never leaves Max alone."

Belinda once again wondered about this supposed romance. Miranda was not exactly discreet about her lukewarm feelings toward her fiancé. If the marriage came off, it would be due to Max's pressure.

The Twins bounded into the dining room, pulled out chairs, waved at the seated participants, ran over to the sideboards and proceeded to load up on Gaston's fabulous bounty. "Wow, this food is great. Hey, you guys have to try those jetskis. They're a real trip."

"We will, if we can get you two out of them."

The kids laughed. "There's six more days. I guess we can let you have a shot at them sometime."

Belinda snorted. "That's very kind of you. I understand we'll be staying here at Lizard Island one more day and then heading south for the Whitsundays. We'll have to get Lucinda to tell us about them when she returns from the resort with her party. As for me, I plan to catch a short nap, sleep off lunch and then back to swimming in the coral. Maybe I can get your father to join in if only with a snorkel."

The others thought a nap was a great idea except of course, for the Twins who were bugging Cameron to refuel the jetskis. They wanted to try the underwater scooters but these were restricted to adults with scuba experience. They would have to become scuba qualified and ecologically briefed before they could zoom along the bottom. Well, they had six more days. Never discouraged.

Chapter Fifteen

The yacht's warned of a quite nasty squall.
Winds and waves and some vicious rainfall.
Max is going to sue
But he isn't sure who
As he gives all his lawyers a call.

Once more, the sound of bear-driven jetskis echoed in the Lizard Island cove. Belinda had talked Octavius into venturing into the scenic waters. They both wore snorkels. Bruce and Tilda were sitting on the deck nursing tropical drinks prepared by Ethan. Miranda was nowhere to be seen.

While the two senior ursines were swimming around, doing underwater sightseeing. the resort Zodiac returned with its six passengers – Lucinda, Geoffrey, the Tigers, Martha and a much annoyed Maximillian. He skittered onto the transom, shedding and dropping his lifejacket in the process.

"The nerve of those Aussie clowns. *(Lucinda winced.)* They wouldn't even consider my offer for one of their villas. Not nearly enough! And we'd have to guarantee a minimum period of residence each year to say nothing of outrageous maintenance fees. Martha is very disappointed. I'm going to get my team of lawyers on them. Nobody snubs 'Makes a Million' Mink and gets away with it." He stomped up the companionway to his stateroom with Geoffrey and Martha picking up the rear."

The Red Fox smiled. "Mr. Mink has a very short fuse and his wife is quite spoiled," she said. "Sorry, I should keep my comments to myself."

Bruce and Tilda laughed. "I guess we're clowns, too. He's a real galah. *(Noisy fool)* No worries, Lucinda, we're on to him. Both of them. I don't know what to make of Geoffrey or Miranda, though."

Lucinda shrugged, "They are bit of a mystery, Inspector. Aside from a few favorable comments about lunch, *(which the yacht paid for and Mad Max dissed)* Geoffrey didn't say a word at the villas. Isn't that right?' She turned to the Tigers for agreement."

Galatea growled and slurped her drink. "Max is a Class A dope, his wife is an over-indulged pain and Geoffrey is a cipher. I thought he was a mute for a while. Altogether, it was not a very pleasant jaunt although the villas and beaches were lovely. The food and drinks were great. But that loud mouth spoiled it all and he's tough to ignore. We'll just have to forget him for the rest of the tour. Oh, look who's emerging from the depths. The polar star of the Some Like it Cold aquatic review and her super-sized mate. Hi Belinda! Hello Octavius!"

The two soggy ursines shook themselves. *(Octavius loved Belinda's wet fur.)* "Well, I thought I'd seen it all. Other worlds, strange beings! I never thought I'd have another new experience but that was well worth the effort and expense and we have six more days. Tell us about Whitehaven Beach and the Whitsundays, Lucinda."

Lucinda passed a bowl of mead to the Great Bear and a large flute of champagne to Belinda. Then she adopted her tour guide voice and did her recitation: "The Whitsundays is an archipelago of 74 tropical islands located just 34 miles off the Queensland coast, next to the Great Barrier Reef. **Whitehaven Beach** is a 4.35 miles stretch along **Whitsunday Island.** Visitors travel to the Whitsundays from all around the world to relax on the pure white silica sands of Whitehaven, soar over Heart Reef and stay in world-class luxury accommodations."

"The clear, protected waters around the island's secluded beaches and hidden bays are ideal for sailing, snorkeling, diving and swimming. The Twins will love it. You Tigers can also fish, if you want to. We'll be heading south to Whitehaven tomorrow evening after another day here. Have you and Ms. Roo been there before, Inspector?"

Bruce said 'yes' and Tilda shook her head 'no.' "Always happy to make a return trip, Lucinda. Whitehaven is a bonzer beach."

They were interrupted by the sound of Max demanding service at the bar. Eyes rolled in unison and then gusts of laughter.

Miranda made an appearance. "Hello, everyone. I see and hear Daddy has returned." She frowned.

A splash of spray hit the transom as the waterborne juveniles came up on the jetskis. "Hi folks! When's dinner?"

Ursula 13 rang her chime and Octavius took up his laptop. "Yes, Ursie?"

"Doctor Bear, sorry to rain on your parade. Literally! But there's a weather report about a freak squall building up off the coast. I thought you should know."

"Thank you! Ursula. Lucinda, has the Captain gotten any reports of a sudden storm coming up?"

"I'll check, Doctor Bear." She keyed in her communicator and listened. "Right-o. Got it."

"I don't know how you discovered that but you're right. The Captain says it's several hours away but it could be a bit nasty. It hasn't shown on our radar yet. We're going to anchor in a sheltered cove here at the island and ride it out. This craft has exceptional resistance to wind and storm water with stabilizers and multiple hulls. But we're not taking any chances. We have to get the Twins off the jetskis and back on board and I'll pass the news on to the rest of the company. The Captain will be on as soon as we have more details."

Bruce shook his head. "Wait till Max hears about this. He'll sue God!" As soon as the Twins were safely back on the yacht, it moved into an inlet surrounded by low lying vegetation. The Captain came on the PA system and announced what we already knew. A storm was brewing. Due in an hour or so just after sundown but not expected to last long. *(They hoped.)*

Out at the bar, another storm was brewing. Max had worked himself up into another rage blaming the upcoming tempest on the

Captain, the yacht rental company, weather reporters, Queensland, Australian climate and yes, God. His lawyers were going to be busy.

Dinner was put on hold. Gaston was beside himself but boncing around in a storm was hardly conducive to good digestion. On the other hand, a few drinks couldn't do any harm and the passengers were helping themselves at the bar while Ethan was otherwise occupied.

Ms. Baker, the emu stewardess and Lucinda were busy securing everything they could in the public areas and helping in the staterooms. Alec, Ethan and Henry had all the loose recreational equipment battened down. They hauled the tenders on board or tied them securely to the hulls. Everyone had donned life jackets. They had actually found one to fit Octavius. It was a reworked flotation pad from the spa.

Cameron was on the bridge with the Captain, maneuvering the boat. Chief Morgan was making sure the engines were performing, the anchors were ready to be dropped and nothing dangerous was loose in the below deck regions. Now if they could only get Max, that loose cannon above decks to shut up. He's a real yobbo.

Max was holding forth to a limited audience. Martha and Geoffrey. Miranda had once again disappeared. He then tried to get Octavius interested in a class-action suit against the tour company but got nowhere. The rest of the group had retreated to their staterooms armed with beverages of choice. The Twins were alternately excited and scared. The Reef Roamer was as ready as it was going to be.

*****

Night and the storm arrived simultaneously. Waves slapped sharply against the hulls of the trimaran. The yacht rocked and pitched and tugged on its anchors. Winds howled, whistled and rattled the now sealed doors, portholes and windows on each level. The antennas twisted and shook. Intense rain pelted the decks in a sharp staccato. Flashes of lightning crackled through the sky followed by rumbling booms of thunder. Mother Nature, Queensland style, was putting on quite a show. Then the vessel went dark except for safety lights. Martha had a fit of booze inspired hysterics. Max cursed.

The Captain announced. "Don't be alarmed. This is only a brief cutover. We're resetting the engines and running the generators to keep the batteries charged. Lights will be on again momentarily." Nevertheless, Martha did her screaming act.

The whole event lasted less than an hour. As rapidly as they had erupted, the winds settled down as the storm passed over on its way south. Cairns was going to get a dowsing. The waves calmed, the rain turned into a mild shower and then stopped. The yacht's lights were back on. In the distance an occasional lightning bolt still flashed and thunder rolled. The storm hadn't finished. It had just moved away.

Stateroom doors opened and the life jacketed incumbents tentatively emerged. The Captain came on. "That seems to have been it, ladies and gentlebeasts. Please keep your life jackets on in case we encounter a stray roller or gust. We're going to stay anchored here for the night. Lucinda, please check on all of our guests and assure that they are OK. Gaston, can you salvage dinner? Ethan, open the bar!"

The Twins were first out of their stateroom. Shook up but as usual, hungry. Belinda and Octavius appeared, followed by the Tigers. Ben growled, "Well, folks, we've flown through lousy weather and gotten knocked around a bit but that was my first ship board storm. Glad we weren't on the open sea. Surrounded by angry water."

Lucinda ran up, her red fox tail waving briskly. "Are all of you alright. No damage, scrapes, bumps or bruises?" Bruce and Tilda had arrived, each with a tin of Foster's. "All present and accounted for, Ma'am. We survived. What about the Minks?"

Max grumbled and tried to raise his lawyers on the satellite phone. Martha sobbed. Miranda was sitting apart and Geoffrey...?

Where was Geoffrey? Nobody knew! Ethan remembered him sitting in the lounge with a drink in each paw, feeling no pain. Then the lights went out. When they came back on, he was gone. Ms. Baker said he wasn't in his room. Did he drunkenly go out into the storm and get blown overboard? No! Ethan found him. Lying face down on the deck next to the overflowing, rain-filled jacuzzi – *He looked very dead!*

Chapter Sixteen

Geoffrey is certainly dead.
It looks like he fell on his head.
Did the wind knock him down?
Was he going to drown?
Or could it be murder instead?

The group was thunderstruck. *(no pun intended)* Another round of hysterics for Martha. She ran off. Ms. Baker, who was also the ship's medical officer, determined that Geoffrey was indeed dead. An accident? Perhaps! Lightweight and very drunk, he may have been knocked over by the wind or tripped and hit his head on the stairs to the jacuzzi. But, to be certain, Chief Inspector Bruce Wallaroo took charge and declared the area a possible crime scene. He had Alec and Henry block it off. "Don't move him. No one touch the body. Call the local police."

The First Officer got on the ship-to-shore phone and called Security at the Lizard Island Resort. He described the situation and requested they put in a call to the police. He also wanted to dock at the resort's slip. They relayed the call and allowed The Reef Roamer to moor at the wharf. The boat maneuvered in the dark with flood lights.

Octavius, Tilda and Belinda gathered round in the dining area. No one was in the mood for food. Even the Twins. Max was making calls on his cell phone and Miranda was sitting quietly in a corner avoiding both her parents. The night progressed.

*****

Morning dawned and a police helicopter from Cairns landed on the sand near the Lizard Island dock. A grey kangaroo and a uniformed wombat emerged from the chopper and advanced toward The Reef Roamer. Detective Inspector McKenzie and Sergeant Ogilvie, both from Cairns Criminal Investigation Division *(CID)*. The Captain stood on the gangplank to greet them along with Bruce and Tilda.

Introductions all around and the two policemen were escorted to the foredeck and the blocked off jacuzzi. The mink's bruised body was still at the foot of the spa, face down and definitely deceased. Ethan told them his story of Geoffrey's disappearance from the lounge. The First Officer described the intensity of the storm and the momentary loss of the lights. The Captain requested the law officers to take the corpse back to Cairns and allow them to continue the voyage.

McKenzie conferred with Bruce and Tilda. He had met her at a conference when she was still on the Melbourne force. They agreed there was little point in holding the superyacht. It certainly looked like a storm induced accident – death by misadventure. The sergeant and Alec lifted the mink's body onto a surfboard and carried it to the helicopter. It would be flown back to the Medical Examiner in Cairns and thence referred to the coroner's office for disposition.

Surprisingly, Max had maintained silence during the whole process. So had Miranda. Martha made up for them by wailing uncontrollably. We felt sure Max would have been full of advice, complaints and demands of all and sundry. Nothing! He was on his phone barking instructions to someone.

The Sergeant asked Max and Miranda about informing Geoffrey's next of kin. Neither one of them knew anyone. Surprising for one's fiancé. McKenzie, Bruce and Tilda all frowned. The police removed Geoffrey's sparse personal effects from his stateroom and loaded them into the chopper.

"We'll be back to you shortly, Skipper. You can resume your tour. Heading to the Whitsundays? We'll be contacting you too, Mr. and Mrs. Mink and Ms. Mink. Please remain available."

They reboarded the helicopter and we watched it head southeast to Cairns. The Twins, who had been standing silently by *(a miracle!)* looked at Ethan and Gaston. "Lunch?"

The engines rumbled and the superyacht reversed itself into the cove. Belinda approached Miranda and said, "I'm so sorry for your

91

loss, Miranda. I suppose you will want to make arrangements for Geoffrey's burial. May we help?"

"No thank you, Bearoness. Geoffrey wasn't my fiancé. He was Max's bodyguard. Max doesn't want it known he needs one. He has a lot of enemies and he's rich. He ordered us to pretend about getting married. It would never have happened. Max's office will take care of the funeral activities."

Belinda gaped and then recovered. "I see. Well then. I'll just mind my own business." She thought, "Wait till our group hears this."

Over drinks that afternoon as we were cruising south from Lizard Island, the team got together out of earshot of the Minks. Belinda passed on Miranda's revelations. This reminded Galatea of a discussion Geoffrey and Max had in the offices of villa management. Max shouted, "I won't be bullied or blackmailed." A classic case of a pot calling a kettle black, considering what a loudmouth tyrant Max was. "Geoffrey just smiled and nodded. Martha interrupted them, whining about wanting to see the model villa." The Tiger thought nothing further about it until Belinda just now mentioned who Geoffrey really was. Tilda frowned and said, "I wonder..!"

The Twins, unable to use the jetskis since the yacht was moving at full speed, challenged the group to a shuffleboard contest.

The Reef Roamer doubled back past Cairns on a heading for the Whitsundays and the pristine Whitehaven Beach. We were in for another surprise. The engines went to idle. A motor launch from Cairns harbor attached itself to the transom of the yacht. Down from the main deck came Alec and Henry carrying the luggage of the Mink family. Martha was crying as usual and Miranda was her stoic self. Max announced. "We're leaving. Glad to get off this ship of doom. Your company will be hearing from my lawyers, Captain. Before you say anything, Inspector Wallaroo, I've checked in with the local police."

Before skittering onto the launch, Miranda stopped and whispered to Belinda. "Just so you know, Max murdered Geoffrey."

Chapter Seventeen

Belinda is stopped in her tracks.
They are learning much more about Max.
If Miranda is right,
The Mink struck in the night.
Was it one of his fearsome attacks?

As the kids would say, "Wow!!" Belinda's mouth dropped as the launch pulled away with its payload of Mustelae and headed back to Cairns harbor. The superyacht started up again. She turned to Octavius who had just been looking on as the Minks departed. "That Miranda is something else. She just accused her father of killing Geoffrey."

He turned to Bruce and Tilda. "Did you hear what Belinda just said?"

Tilda spoke up first. "We have to talk with McKenzie."

Bruce replied, "Hold on. Let's think this through. Why did she tell Belinda and not one of us. After all, we're the police."

Octavius pawsed for a second and said, "She wasn't sure what our reaction would be. She wanted time to disappear. Want to bet Max never contacted McKenzie to tell him they're leaving the yacht? I assume they still have their passports and can leave Australia any time they want. Why do you think she told you, Bel?"

The Bearoness replied, "I think I'm the only one she trusted. You two are the law. Octavius is a detective and the Tigers are pilots."

Tilda chimed in, "She may be a nut. She obviously hates Max. Her mother is in a drunken haze most of the time. A real whinger."

Belinda said, "Miranda may not be their real daughter."

"Welcome to Fantasyland."

"No, I'm serious. The whole situation is really bizarre."

The Great Bear hesitated. "Let's get another brain working on this. Ursula, have you been following the action?"

"Yes, Doctor Bear. I've been in passive mode all morning. Listening, collecting and analyzing data. Ms. Miranda is quite unusual. Max and Martha are not. He's a moneyed thug and she's a sot. He's quite ruthless. I've done further research on him and uncovered a number of instances where he has exercised highly questionable tactics to get what he wanted. As you know, he also has a fierce temper."

Belinda asked, "Do you think he's capable of murder?"

"Yes, Bearoness, I do. Either by himself or hiring someone. That would be more his style. I also think he's capable of money laundering."

"Oh, come on. That would be too much of a coincidence."

"Not really. As we found out, The Amalgamated Bank has an extensive list of questionable clients in a wide range of countries. Max and his businesses fit the AUSTRAC profile. Some of his biggest customers are fronts for terror organizations. Engines keep wars running. It might actually be why he's in Australia. They came up from Melbourne. I think he was at the bank."

Octavius turned to Bruce and Tilda. "OK, we need to call McKenzie. At a minimum, we have to get him to prevent the Minks from leaving the country at least until the coroner makes his decision. You know McKenzie, Bruce. Can you share our suspicions about Geoffrey's death being murder? Let's not mention Miranda's comment to Bel just yet if we can help it. "

"He may be tough to convince but he's not going to like Max's defying him. He can at least put a team on them at Cairns Airport. I'll call now."

The great Bear smiled. "I could use a mead. Anyone for shuffleboard?"

Belinda sucked in her breath. "I need a champagne. Where's Ethan?"

Lucinda popped in, holding drink bowls. "Sorry, Ethan doesn't seem to be available. Will I do?"

Henry came up and said, "Hey, Ms. Lucinda. I saw Ethan getting on that launch for Cairns. Did you send him into town for something? He didn't say anything to any of us."

Octavius looked at Bruce. "Are you thinking what I'm thinking?"

"I'll put in another call to McKenzie. Lucinda, tell the Captain Ethan has gone AWOL."

The Captain was not pleased.

*****

As the Reef Roamer plowed along southward, First Officer Cameron came on the PA after breakfast and announced. "Our next stop is Magnetic Island. Or Maggie Island, if you want to sound like a local. We'll anchor in Horseshoe Bay where you can kayak, jetski, scuba, surfboard and fish from our tender. The coral population is much smaller there but the waters are marvelously clear. If you would like to do a little land exploring, we can set you up with a beach excursion. Maggie Island also has a number of hotels and campsites."

"Oh, by the way. There are no magnetic anomalies. The name came about when Captain Cook, the great British explorer lion, had trouble with his ship's compass as he charted the island. He believed there was some magnetic property affecting the device. No one has been able to reproduce the effect since but the name stuck. Please let Lucinda know what your recreational intentions are. Thank you."

Lucinda appeared in the dining room and circulated among the eight remaining passengers. The Tigers wanted to fish. The Twins decided they wanted to try kayaks leaving the jetskis for the adults. Bruce and Tilda chose to give the powered seahorses a try. Belinda, a skilled scuba and underwater performer opted for a submerged run with a scooter. The Great Bear settled down for a session with Ursula. *(He didn't reveal her identity to any of the yacht's crew. The passengers, of course, were aware of her.)*

"Bruce, any news from McKenzie.

"Yeah, he tracked down the Minks and made them turn over their passports until the coroner makes his decision. Max is threatening another lawsuit."

"Why am I not surprised. What about Ethan?"

"He's still at large. He knows his way round Cairns and may well have skipped town altogether. He's certainly brought a lot of suspicion on himself."

Octavius agreed, "I got the impression he was not too bright. But probably greedy. I don't know what he makes on this boat. The tips are probably good but unpredictable. Just the sort of character Max would have been able to bribe or squeeze. My guess is while the lights were out. he pushed the drunken Geoffrey out onto the deck and down the stairs and then slugged him. The battering from the storm did the rest. Do you think Geoffrey was blackmailing Max?"

"Judging from that argument that the Tigers picked up, I'd say it's highly likely."

"This whole trip is turning out to be a tale out of True Crime Stories."

"I told you, you wouldn't retire."

"Don't say that in front of Belinda."

"Hardly. Not gonna risk another barney with a polar bear."

"Do you think we should notify AUSTRAC about Ursula's suspicions of Max and money laundering?"

"You betcha, Ursula's suspicions are usually certainties."

Chapter Eighteen

Say hello to the Magnetic Isle
You can swim and cavort in grand style.
With the exit of Max
Now they all can relax.
The Great Bear even broke out a smile.

The Reef Roamer anchored in Horseshoe Bay at Magnetic Island and another day of waterborne fun and games began…at least for some of them.

Bruce had been in contact with AUSTRAC and they had requested that he go to Cairns, find Max Mink and face him down about money laundering through the Amalgamated Bank of Melbourne. A helicopter from the Townsville Police Department landed on the beach and the Roamer's tender took Bruce and Tilda to the shore. They boarded and the whirlybird rose up and headed northwest to Cairns, 216 miles away. The Twins watched as it chattered off.

McTavish asked, "Where are Uncle Bruce and Tilda going, Dad?"

"Up to Cairns. They'll be back in time for a late dinner."

"What's in Cairns besides our airplane?"

"Not what! Who! Max Mink and the two ladies. He's under police surveillance. They've taken their passports. Max is fighting back."

"Do you think he killed Geoffrey?"

"We don't know. Bruce wants to talk with him about something else. Money laundering!

"Washing money? That sounds crazy."

"Not literally. It means disguising money used in a crime."

"He's a criminal? I thought so. Bella and I don't like him. We don't like any of them. His wife is a hysterical pain and Miranda is just plain weird."

"Well, we'll see what Bruce uncovers. Are you guys taking the kayaks?"

"Yeah, you can have the jetskis today. The Tigers are going fishing."

"Thank you! Very generous of you."

He laughed, "Think nothing of it. Mom's going to use the underwater scooter. She's scuba qualified and a capable pilot."

"She's more than capable. She's an expert."

"Well, I'm an expert eater and I haven't had breakfast yet."

*****

The helicopter's engines and vibrating rotors made conversation difficult so Bruce and Tilda resorted to texting. They had Ursula installed on the Wallaroo's lap top and a three way discussion was in progress. Fortunately, the police chopper had internet capability, so the AGI could access the cloud-based records as they moved along.

"Ursula, you definitely have Max tied into a laundering scheme?"

"Oh, yes. His paws are all over the transactions. Working through intermediaries, he's supplying engines and replacement parts to several warlords in Africa and Afghanistan who are under international sanctions. They pay mostly with gem stones or precious metals that are then sold on illicit markets and the proceeds deposited in fake accounts in several countries, including Australia."

"As you know, it is illegal to open a bank account here under a false name. Comprehensive due diligence must be performed when new bank accounts are opened. That's where AUSTRAC has jumped on Amalgamated Bank. Phony accounts. But it's not easy to trace the actual clients. Encrypted entries, blind transactions, and substitute entities. It gave our Deep Data folks a real challenge to track them but they made great inroads. AUSTRAC has its evidence and "Makes a Million" Max is definitely one of the offenders."

"Do you think Geoffrey was blackmailing Max over the money laundering?"

"I can't be sure but I think it was likely. This thing about being Miranda's fiancé just didn't smell right. I think he started out as Max's bodyguard but saw an opportunity to cash in."

"So, Ursula, you think Max had Geoffrey killed and Ethan is the likely killer."

"My probability algorithms give it a very high rating but no certainty. We don't believe the death was an accident."

Bruce typed, "Neither do I nor the Cairns police. McKenzie is trying very hard to track down Ethan. We'll see if he's made any progress when we arrive."

*****

Back in Horseshoe Bay, Captain Fergus approached Octavius and Belinda. "G'day Doctor and Bearoness. Feeling magnetic here at Maggie? We leave for Whitehaven tomorrow. Are you and your party enjoying your tour?"

Octavius snorted, "Very much so and things have improved even more dramatically with the departure of the Minks."

The more diplomatic Bearoness replied, "Oh yes, Captain, The Barrier Reef is fabulous and so is your ship. The food, drinks and wine are exquisite. The rooms are lovely. All the diversions you could possibly want and the crew is exceptional. I'm so glad we booked with your company. We made it through that storm with flying colors. Well, most of us made it."

The Captain hopped slightly on one foot. "That's the first death we've had on the Roamer. I hope it's the last."

Octavius looked at him. "Do you think it was an accident?"

"I'd like to believe that but I'm having trouble with Ethan's disappearance. Not at all like him. He was very carefully vetted. A real mystery. He was a great bartender, too. I hate to lose him. Of course, his departure may be totally unconnected."

"The police are searching for him."

"I know. Inspector McKenzie has been on to me several times about it. I gave him Ethan's address in Cairns but most of the time he was aboard the Reef Roamer. We have a very heavy schedule. When we take you back we have only twenty four hours to do a turnaround. I'm doing a stem to stern checkup. I don't think we took any damage from the storm. No lightning hits. A broken vase or two. A few of Gaston's pots got a dent. The jacuzzi is back in service and the guest cruising equipment is all good."

"Great! We're looking forward to several more pleasant days, especially with Max Mink gone."

"Do you think that pommie wally is going to sue?"

"I suspect he's going to be a bit busy. He's in real trouble with Australia and several other governments. Fraudulent financial transactions."

"I better inform the company. Fortunately, he paid in advance and we settled the balance before he left. We'd better check his credit."

Belinda chimed in, "Lucinda has been doing a great job and now she's also substituting for Ethan. This boat seems to have an endless supply of champagne. Well, so long! I'm off to the scooters."

The Captain laughed. "We did a little research on your group's culinary and liquid preferences, Bearoness. It took a little doing to find mead for you, Doctor Bear. I hope you like it."

"Ambrosia, Captain. I brought my own supply aboard but I haven't touched it. Thank you!"

Chapter Nineteen

Bruce and Tilda catch up with the Minks.
Max's action, as usual, stinks.
Though he bellows and screams.
He's a fraud, so it seems.
He is just not as tough as he thinks.

Cairns: The unmarked police SUV turned into the Pullman Reef Hotel Casino entrance area. Tilda whistled. "He's not cutting back on his luxuries, is he."

Bruce bounced out of the car and headed past the liveried doorman into the opulent lobby with two uniformed constables in tow. He flashed his warrant card at the concierge and asked for the manager. The goat stared at him and Tilda, bleated softly and reached for the phone. "I hope nothing untoward has taken place, Inspector."

"Nothing that need concern you or your management."

A brown Australian Stock Horse emerged from his office, nodded at the concierge and said, "Thank you, Gary." He turned to the law officers *(Yes we know, Tilda's in private practice.)* and looked at Bruce's warrant card. "You're a long way from Melbourne, Inspector. Nothing amiss locally, I hope. By the way, I'm Steven Stock, Manager of the Pullman Reef Hotel Casino. How can I help?"

"You have a small family of Minks in residence here, Mr. Stock. Maximilian Mink, his wife and daughter."

"I'm well aware of it, Inspector. He's been in my office filing complaints ever since he arrived. If it's not the hotel, it's the casino. He's accused us of running a dishonest roulette wheel. We've also had to cut off his wife's bar tab. She could barely stand. The daughter seems OK. I'm on the verge of kicking them out but they're occupying one of our top luxury suites, paid in advance. The hotel owners would not be pleased. He's a very affluent industrialist from the UK."

"He's also a crook. We're here to arrest him. Where is he?"

The Horse whinnied. "Aha! I wondered about him. At this time of day, you'll probably find him in the casino. He's a compulsive gambler and a compulsive loser."

As they moved away from the front desk, he asked, "What has he done?"

"International, large scale fraud and money laundering. That's all I can tell you. Now, will you lead us to the casino?"

"Certainly, since he doesn't trust the roulette, you'll probably find him pounding away at the 100 dollar pokie machines although I'm sure he thinks they're fixed, too."

Sure enough, perched high on a stool, Max was frantically pressing buttons and screaming at the screens that kept turning up useless payouts. He didn't notice the legal entourage approaching him.

"Hello, Max! Fancy meeting you here."

The Mink looked up, startled. It took him several seconds to recover. "Inspector Wallaroo is it? And Enquiry Agent Tilda? Why aren't you on the Reef Roamer? Did you get tired of looking at coral? Why are these two constables with you?"

"I think you know why, Max. I'm sure your cronies at the Amalgamated Bank of Melbourne have warned you about AUSTRAC's crackdown."

"AUSTRAC? What's AUSTRAC? What are you talking about?"

"I'm talking about fraud and money laundering, Max. You're wanted in several countries including the UK. I'm taking you into custody on behalf of the Australian government. Constables, please take him. I'll read you your rights. You already know what they are."

"This is absurd. I insist on contacting my lawyers. I'll sue you for false arrest."

"You do that. By the way, I'm returning to the yacht tonight."

*****

The Police SUV with the loudly protesting Max Mink, pulled up to the parking facility behind Cairns District Police Headquarters. At the hotel, Max had been allowed to tell Martha and Miranda that he was being unjustly abducted by the Queensland authorities. Martha, in typical fashion threw a hysterical fit. Tilda thought she saw Miranda stifle a grin. Max told her to alert his law firm.

Inspector McKenzie greeted them and took the Mink into custody. Max protested nonstop, invoking his lawyers as well as his judicial and government cronies both here and in the UK. "You'll regret this, Wallaroo. You, too McKenzie. Your badges and warrant cards will be in the dunny forever. And then I'll sue you personally for all you're worth for false arrest."

"You're entitled to one phone call, Max. I suggest you use it. Your lawyers in England probably have an affiliation with some of the criminal lawyers her in Cairns. Or has your daughter already made the connection."

"You wait. I'll be out of here in nothing flat and then heaven help you Gestapo bullies." The constables led him off to a holding cell.

McKenzie turned to Bruce and Tilda. "How tight is the case against him?"

"AUSTRAC is satisfied they have enough to indict him and the UK National Economic Crime Centre (NECC); National Crime Agency (NCA) and the UK Financial Intelligence Unit have invoked the Criminal Finances Act of 2018 against him. The NCA has originated Unexplained Wealth Orders (UWOs) to allow recovery of criminal assets related to Max's business interests. They've also successfully issued a number of Account Freezing Orders to hold millions of pounds in his accounts. He's going to be tied up for quite a while. His lawyers may be able to get him released but we still have his passport. Remember, he's also a person of interest in Geoffrey's death. His daughter has accused him to Belinda but not to us. It's useless."

McKenzie said, "Miranda wants her passport back. She wants to return to the UK. It doesn't seem to bother her to leave her mother here alone while we have Max in custody."

Bruce pondered. "You know, the Bearoness may be right. She may not be their daughter. Or maybe she's adopted. Let's give the two of them back their passports and tell them they're free to go. We'll see what happens."

Tilda piped up. "Any news on the Ethan front? Is he still our number one suspect? I think we all agree that was no accident. "

McKenzie snorted. "Too many sightings. All dingoes look alike to me."*(Not true. They vary in size and coloration. Ethan was a sturdy brown with a scar on his snout.)* Bruce didn't challenge him but was somewhat dubious about them catching up with Ethan.

"Well, Tilda and I are heading back to Magnetic Island and the Reef Roamer. I leave Max up to you. No, no. Don't thank me. Put him in a soundproof cell until his lawyers come to bail him out. Let me know if you run Ethan down. A pity that! He mixed a great Martini."

Back to the airport, the police helicopter and another 216 mile trip back to Magnetic Island and the superyacht.

Underwater scooters or DPVs *(Diver Propulsion Vehicles.)* have little or no relationships to jetskis. You don't ride on them. You hold on to them in the depths, steer and they pull you along. They're battery powered and vary dramatically from type to type in speed, depth of operation and size of diver. Needless to say, the Reef Roamer was equipped with top of the line units.

Belinda had spent the afternoon in her scuba gear being drawn along the waters around Magnetic Island while the Twins were kayaking. Wonder of wonders! Octavius and the two Tigers went fishing. Dinner would wait until Bruce and Tilda returned.

Chapter Twenty

Where is Ethan? They all want to know.
When he left where the heck did he go?
And Miranda, who's she?
What can she really be?
Is her daughter routine just for show?

Angelfish, clownfish, damselfish, parrotfish and other decorative varieties got caught and tossed back by Octavius and the Tigers. Groupers galore. Gaston had asked them to try and catch a coral trout – good for dinner. They did but had to elude a shark who had similar ideas. All told, an interesting but not particularly restful afternoon on the Reef Roamer's tender.

As expected, the Twins got to use their life jackets several times when they capsized their kayaks, laughing uncontrollably. Were kayaks going to join jetskis in the Polar Paradise aquatic inventory? Probably. Harold was in for a serious upgrade in equipment.

Belinda was working on her first *(but hardly last)* champagne of the day when Lucinda, substitute bartender, asked, "Bearoness. How was the scuba experience today?"

"Lovely! Less coral then Lizard Island but fish and turtles aplenty. I'm looking forward to Whitehaven Beach. Do you ever get to dive and engage in watersports or is it all business?"

"Usually I'm too busy but with those Minks gone, I might get a chance. We foxes aren't crazy about swimming and I don't like the water very much but I must confess those jetskis are a lot of fun. If only I could figure out how to use them without getting wet. Your tigers seem to share my aversion. And now, of course, I'm doing permanent bartender duty with Ethan gone."

"You know, we can serve ourselves. We all know how to open a bottle and pour. The Twins know how to make smoothies, too."

"Thanks for the offer but Captain Fergus would never approve. Service is his watchword."

"Speaking of Ethan, do you think he killed Geoffrey the Mink."

"I don't know. I hope not but I can't explain his skedaddling like that."

"As she left, Miranda whispered to me that Max killed Geoffrey. I don't know if she meant he actually did the deed or hired someone, maybe Ethan, to do it."

"That's a strange thing for a daughter to say. If she is his daughter."

"What do you mean, Lucinda?"

"That group piqued my curiosity to say nothing of my annoyance. I understand Inspector Wallaroo and Ms. Matilda went to Cairns to arrest Max. Was that for Geoffrey's murder?"

"No, he seems to be involved in large scale money laundering. That's why he's in custody. But what did you mean about Miranda?"

The Fox replied, "I did a little investigation myself. There are no records of Max and Martha Mink having a daughter. I think she's a fraud. You know what I think. She's their maid. That wife doesn't seem to take a sober breath and probably needs someone to take care of her. I'd be angry if I had that job."

"That's rich. It seems Geoffrey wasn't Miranda's fiancé. He was Max's bodyguard."

"Strewth! No wonder Miranda didn't seem enthused about getting married to Geoffrey. They were quite a group. Maybe drunken Martha is really the brains behind the outfit." She laughed.

Belinda frowned "I'll believe anything about them."

Octavius arrived at that moment. "What'll you believe about whom."

"The Minks. They're all phonies."

Lucinda trotted off and returned shortly with a jug of mead for the Great Bear. She then refilled Belinda's champagne bowl and turned to see the Tigers emerging from Gaston's kitchen.

"Ooh, did you catch some fish for Gaston? He makes a super trout with orange-saffron sauce."

"Well, he now has a prime candidate." Galatea giggled and took one of the glasses of Scotch that Lucinda held out.

Ben joined in. "Thanks, Lucinda. Any news about Ethan?"

"Still missing as far as we know."

The Tiger went on. "You know. There was something strange about those Minks. When they were at the Lizard Island villas, I got the distinct impression none of them were who they said they were. Except maybe Max. He couldn't resist showing off his wealth. But I guess all you get on these cruises are animals with more money than sense. Oops! Present company excepted, of course."

Belinda smiled and nodded, "No offense taken, Ben. But what struck you."

"Miranda and Geoffrey! Getting married? Not likely! She looked like she hated the guy. And Martha. She sobered up pretty quickly when they started negotiating for a villa. I think she was faking all the hysteria and drunkenness. I don't know. That female just set my whiskers to twitching."

The cubs burst on the scene. "Kayaks! We need them. Can you get Harold to order up at least a pair, Mom. Along with jetskis. The North Sea would be a great place for watersports. The guests at Polar Paradise would love them."

"Oh, they'd be for the guests, huh. I don't suppose you'd get any use out of them."

"Well, maybe now and then and of course, there's Otto, too."

Chapter Twenty One

Off they go on their aerial tour
To Heart Reef, that great sign of amour.
Then they'll fly down to reach
Famous Whitehaven Beach
With its waters and sand both so pure.

The sun was descending as the Townsville Police helicopter flew over the superyacht and landed on the Horseshoe Bay beach. Alerted by the chopper pilot of their arrival, Alec steered the tender to the sandy stretch and picked up the two stalwarts of the law.

Lucinda stood on the transom deck holding out two cans of Foster's. *(It's never drunk from a glass.)*

Bruce bounded aboard followed by Tilda. He grabbed the beer, took a healthy swig, wiped his mouth and said, "Thanks Lucinda, I needed that."

Ms. Roo hopped on in ladylike fashion and took the offered tinny sedately in her paws and gave it a mighty swallow. What a pair!

"Our friend Max is in the Cairns pokey waiting for transfer to Melbourne and the two females have their passports back. We're waiting to see what they do. McKenzie is keeping a careful eye on them. No results about Ethan. The search goes on. When's dinner?"

McTavish ran out on the deck and shouted, "Hi, Uncle Bruce! Hi, Aunt Tilda. We've been waiting dinner for you. Gaston's done another treat. Hurry up! We're starving! *(So, what else is new?)*

As dinner began, the Reef Roamer powered up and began its journey to the Whitsundays. First stop, Airlie Beach. They sailed along in a starlit night. No storms or choppy seas. A few postprandial drinks, laugh filled conversation with Bruce telling one ridiculous story after another and Octavius chiming in and then off to bed and some glorious mink-free sleep.

*****

The Bearoness had booked a seaplane tour to fly over Heart Reef and Whitehaven next morning. Octavius, who wouldn't fit comfortably in the plane, chose to stay aboard the yacht and catch up with the Octavians in Cincinnati, courtesy of Ursula 13. The Twins and Tigers opted to join Bruce, Tilda and Belinda in the plane.

The roar of the de Havilland DHC-3T Turbo Otter floatplane's engine as it taxied and maneuvered up to the superyacht's transom killed off any conversation. The engine and prop then idled. Alec and Henry gave the passengers a boost as they clambered up the ladders on the twin pontoons and into the fuselage. Belinda sat up front in the co-pilot seat and introduced herself to the emu pilot. She informed him that he had three pilots aboard, none of whom had ever flown or even been in a floatplane.

"It's a bit different. The pontoons affect performance, increasing drag and weight and on takeoff and landing, the water provides resistance. Our takeoff runs are longer and we need full power to break loose. Landing's a bit easier but also requires full power to avoid being flipped by waves. Like anything in aviation, it's an acquired skill that takes a lot of practice. Once we're airborne, we'll be moving at a fairly slow speed courtesy of the drag but that works out well for sightseeing. If everybody's belted in, we can get going. Heart Reef first and then Whitehaven Beach."

He pulled away from the yacht and taxied slowly out to a clear reef-free space to make his take off run. Belinda and the Tigers watched him with professional interest. Bruce, as usual, fidgeted in his seat, willing the plane to fly. Tilda just relaxed and looked out the windows as the spray began to build around the plane. The tail dropped as the turboprop equipped nose gradually pointed skyward. The Twins were mesmerized. Suddenly the floats broke loose of the water's grip and the Otter smoothly ascended to a cruising altitude and the views of Airlie Beach, the Heart Reef and Whitehaven.

Heart Reef

Heart Reef, near Airlie Beach, is a stunning composition of coral that amazingly, has naturally formed into the shape of a heart. It has become a major tourist attraction and photographers from around the world have captured it primarily from the air. Fortunately, air traffic was sparse that morning as the Turbo Otter approached and circled the reef.

The Twins busied themselves taking pictures with their professional grade movie and still cameras. *(Used primarily in creating scenes and effects for their Internet games.)* Tilda settled for her cell phone's wide angle lens. The young bears had been creating a pictorial history of their trip and had accumulated a massive photographic library out on the UUI cloud. Arabella had plans for producing a short feature film – working title: Bears Down Under. The Heart Reef would occupy prime space. Belinda split her attention between the Reef and the emu's flying techniques. She was greatly impressed by both.

On to Hill Inlet and Whitehaven Beach, its clear turquoise waters paired with pure white silica sand stretching 4 1/3 miles around the inlet. While they were flying over it, the Reef Roamer was sailing at full speed toward the same destination. The plane would intercept the yacht and return its passengers in time for a late lunch. They would be on the move again and anchor near the beach and personally experience the waters and sand. The beach was carefully controlled to maintain its pristine beauty. Kayaks were OK. As were Jetskis and water skis. But messes weren't tolerated.

*****

It was crowded on the bridge of the superyacht, caused primarily by the oversized presence of Octavius. The Captain and First Officer were piloting the boat. Lucinda was checking radar, broadcasting their position and destination and listening for the floatplane. Suddenly Captain Fergus' cellphone rang. He listened, nodded, listened some more and said "I understand. Thank you, Ethan. See you when we dock at Cairns."

Octavius, Lucinda and First Officer Cameron all stared at him. "That was Ethan."

The Great Bear snorted. "I gathered that. Where is he? What's the story?"

"He's in Cairns. He called to tell me he's quitting his job with us and signing on as a bartender in one of the top tier hotels. It seems he's married.'

"So what? Explain, please."

Lucinda smiled. 'All of our staff are single. This yacht doesn't have enough crew space for wives, husbands and families. And we sail day in and out - practically around the clock. Living on shore just doesn't work."

The Captain continued. "It seems Ethan figured out a way to keep a wife while working on the Reef Roamer. I don't know how he did it. But she just had pups. That's why he took off in the tender. He needed to be with her full time."

"Has this happened before?"

Lieutenant Cameron replied, "Once or twice. Other crew members. How they had enough time to have an affair is beyond me."

"But what does that say about his guilt or innocence in Geoffrey's death?"

"He swears he had nothing to do with the Mink's murder, if it was murder. When the power failed, he left the bar and using his cell phone light, went looking for auxiliary lamps and flashlights for you passengers. When the power came back on, he was on the main deck with a stack of flashes in his paws. I believe him. He may have kept his marital status a secret but Ethan is an honest dingo. He's no killer even though dingoes have their ferocious moments."

"So you're willing to accept his claim of innocence. I'm afraid that's not going to be enough for the Cairns constabulary."

"Maybe not but what's that old story of innocent until proven guilty. We believe in that here is Australia. I doubt he can afford it so I'll spring for lawyer for him. He was a loyal crew member. The company may find its way to support him. It still has to be proven it was murder."

"Yes, there is that. Well, we're back to square one. Let's wait for Inspector Wallaroo to return before contacting McKenzie to call off the search. At least we know where Ethan is. I doubt he'll be taking off anywhere. We'll want to talk with him when we get back to Cairns."

Chapter Twenty Two

Now we know where young Ethan has gone.
Is Ms. Martha's drunk act a put on?
Is Miranda a sham?!
Is she pulling a scam?
It's a lie-filled, conspired marathon!

The turboprop floatplane banked gracefully over the superyacht, waggled its wings and began the long descent onto the waters near Airlie Beach. The Reef Roamer had just arrived in the Whitsundays and was preparing to reclaim its passengers. Lucinda and the pilot were in active radio conversation.

The Twins were filming the superyacht as they passed over and settled back to watch the landing. Belinda was observing how the emu controlled the engine and flaps. Touching the surface first with the trailing edge of the pontoons and slowly dropping into full contact with the tranquil water, the floatplane coasted to a near stop.

"Well done. You can always tell a real pro."

The emu responded. "Thanks Bearoness, but the surface was very calm today and this airplane is quite stable. I've made rougher landings. Now let's get you and your companions back to the Reef Roamer. Just in time for lunch. By the way, my sister is Ms. Baker, your stewardess. Did you all enjoy the flight?"

High fives from the Twins. Appreciative growls from the Tigers and applause from Belinda, Tilda and Bruce. The emu, whose name they didn't know, boosted the throttle and headed back to the waiting vessel. Alec and Henry were standing by to haul them aboard. Octavius was standing on the transom, a cask of mead in his paw.

As Belinda landed on the deck, Lucinda shouted, "Welcome back!" Wagging her capacious fox tail. "We have news. Ethan has reappeared. He was in Cairns all the time." She proceeded to tell the Bearoness, Tilda and Bruce the circumstances of Ethan's vanishing and then vanished herself into the bowels of the yacht. Over her shoulder, she said, "I have to arrange for Ethan's replacement. I'm no bartender."

Bruce wiggled his ears, "Well, he doesn't seem to be a criminal fugitive but he's still a suspect for Geoffrey's killing. I'll call McKenzie and update him. Anything new on those two female minks?"

Octavius shook his head. "We haven't heard anything. Max is on his way to Melbourne and an indictment but those two are still in Cairns. They're a strange pair. I think Belinda is right. Miranda is Martha's maid and Martha has been faking her hysterics and drunkenness. The question is 'why?'"

Tilda answered, "To appear the helpless, brainless female incapable of plotting or carrying out a murder. It's a clever act. I think Max was their primary target but first they had to get rid of his bodyguard. Then a change in plans. Don't kill Max. Frame him for Geoffrey's death. Remember Miranda told Belinda Max was a murderer. But then the money laundering situation kicked in. Max has a date with the law. They didn't expect that but it actually may get him out of their way."

Belinda frowned, "But she was living in the lap of luxury. Did you see all those diamonds. Why frame him or worse yet, dispose of him. She had everything she could want."

Octavius responded, "But at what price? I think she hates Max. So does Miranda. He's a tyrant. Could you live with him? Martha probably has someone else. Bruce, can you get McKenzie to keep them from leaving town?"

The Wallaroo replied. "Yes, I can. But hold on, my bonzer buddies. I have never heard such a pile of suppositions. I respect your opinions but that's all they are – opinions. A few facts would help."

Octavius snorted and said, "Let's get our fact finder active." He tapped his laptop and brought Ursula on line."

"Hello, Doctor Bear. I was wondering when you were going to summon me. I've been running along in passive mode so I'm up to date on the Ethan situation and I've listened to all your opinions about the Minks. I've done some in depth research on Martha and Miranda."

Bruce took another slug of his beer and sputtered, "What have you got, Ursie?"

"Well, first you should know that Martha is chairwoman of Mink Industries. She's hardly the hysterical drunk she pretends to be. "

"What!!"

"She's a silent front for Max who no doubt was afraid that his financial chicanery would eventually unravel. He appears on the organization charts of several of his subsidiaries but he has no corporate presence at the top of the conglomerate. She does. I believe Max's strategy is about to backfire."

"She's been in contact with their corporate lawyers and is about to give evidence to AUSTRAC in exchange for freedom from prosecution. She's accusing Max individually of money laundering as well as fraud. If the indictments stick, she could end up running what's left of the company. Of course, there's a Board of Directors and stockholders to contend with but she's a very formidable female. She may well pull it off."

Belinda asked, "What was with the drunk act?"

"I believe that was for Max's benefit. She wanted to convince him she was no longer competent. He fell for it. His ego is too great to take her as a serious threat."

Tilda whistled. "She must really hate the guy."

The AGI continued. "There are rumors that she has been having an affair with one of the Directors. They may have plotted this out together."

"What about Miranda?"

"She's Martha's personal secretary, not her maid. I believe she has been propositioned by Max several times. She told him to get lost."

"Another member of the 'Makes a Million' fan club."

"It seems so. He's built up quite a population of enemies."

Bruce pondered. "This is all very interesting but it still doesn't tell us who killed Geoffrey, why or whether it was murder at all."

Ursula responded, "The 64,000 dollar question! *(87,271.04 Australian dollars.)* I'm on less reliable ground on that one. In the words of Sherlock Holmes, 'Data, data, data!' We need more information. As you say, Inspector. Opinions won't do!"

Octavius turned to the Wallaroo. "Can McKenzie hold them until we get back to Cairns?"

"Not sure. They have a couple of pretty sharp local lawyers working away to get them unblocked and back to the UK. However, the flights to London do not leave Cairns every day and none of them are direct. The principal airlines do a stopover in Tokyo. Japan is a member of Interpol and if necessary, I can call on their National Police Agency to intercept them when they land. That is, if we believe we have evidence against them."

The Great Bear mused, "Well, let's see if McKenzie comes up with anything. Maybe Ethan can shed some light on the affair. Meanwhile, I'm for exploring that exquisite beach. I may even water ski or wakeboard. Have to do it at least once before we leave the Reef."

Belinda winced. She always worried about Octavius' narcolepsy. She would need to join him and make sure he could handle the skis or board. At nine feet tall, standing erect, his center of gravity was different. Of course, he could ride on all fours, provided they found a board long enough."

"OK, Tavi. Let's get your improvised life jacket and find out what Alec and Henry can come up with in the way of water skis."

Chapter Twenty Three

It's the Reef Roamer's last day at sea
And the group is as hyped as can be.
The Great Bear flipped and soared
On a tandem wakeboard
And the Twins once again got to ski.

The crew of the Reef Roamer were trying hard to hold back their mirth as Octavius struggled to get on a pair of water skis. The Twins showed no such restraint.

"Dad, use the wakeboard on all fours. You won't be able to keep your balance standing upright on the water skis. You're too tall. You'll tilt over. "

"Thanks for your confidence, Arabella."

Belinda tried not to laugh. "Tavi, she's right. This time, your height is defeating you. Your center of gravity needs to be lowered. You're a physicist. You know this stuff. Going on all fours is the way to do it. And no acrobatics! You'll kill yourself. You'll need a helmet."

The Great Bear looked helplessly at Alec and Henry. "Have you guys got something I can use?"

Henry replied. "I think so, Doctor Bear. We keep an oversize board for the daredevils who want to ride tandem. It should work for you. We need to find you a helmet."

"Never mind. I have one in my luggage. I use it to ride my large motorcycle back in Cincinnati. I don't know why I packed it for this trip but it may have its use here."

"That's dinky-di! We'll get the board. You get the helmet and then we'll take out the speedboat. And you Twins. No buzzing him with the jetskis. This your father we're talkin' about."

McTavish chortled, "Aw, Gee, Henry! you're no fun."

Belinda frowned at them. "No fooling around."

It was not unusual for the beach denizens on Whitehaven to observe an animal parasailing or jetskiing or surfboarding on the turquoise waters. What they had never seen before was a nine foot Kodiak on all fours wake boarding behind a sleek speedboat. An audience built up on the shore watching this phenomenon with amazement and with some applause.

"Who's next, Shirley. An elephant?"

Octavius had managed to get astride and then up on the extra-large wakeboard and was holding his own at the end of the tow rope.

The Twins were sitting in their motionless jetskis watching the proceedings and Belinda was poised on the deck of the slowly cruising tender ready to jump in if he fell over asleep. No such problem arose and after several rounds in the inlet, the speedboat returned to the yacht. The Great Bear came close to falling over into the water as he reached for the transom deck. But ursine dignity was preserved.

The Twins started up their motorized seahorses and raced off. Tilda, Bruce, Belinda and the Flying Tigers had been on the tender watching Octavius. The little boat moved toward the Reef Roamer and a round of celebratory thirst quenchers.

Lucinda rolled a drinks table onto the transom and began handing out beverages of choice and snacks to the adult participants.

Bruce held up Arabella's movie camera and laughed, "Well. Ocko. That's all been captured for posterity and is on its way to the UUI cloud. You may want to negotiate with your daughter to keep it out of her feature film."

"Blackmail from my own flesh and blood. Which reminds me, Bruce. Did we ever determine if Geoffrey was a blackmailer?"

"No, we didn't although that outburst of Max's at the villa sounds like he believed it."

"Did he? He may have been talking to Geoffrey about someone else. Maybe Miranda or Martha or some one in his company. That's all Galatea heard, isn't it? Let's call Gal and ask her." The Bear reached for his phone.

Bruce replied. "Yeah, Martha interrupted the discussion. She wanted to see a villa. Or maybe not."

"You're very suspicious of the lady."

"Darn right I am. Like her husband, she's a phony and Ursula has proof."

"Well let's make sure McKenzie keeps them here until we can get back. Meanwhile, I'm for another mead and getting ready for our final dinner on the Reef Roamer."

The White Tiger came onto the deck. "Galatea, sorry to disturb you but we wanted you to settle something for us."

"Sure, Doctor Bear. What's up?"

"Remember your trip to the Lizard Island villas?"

A nod!

"Remember you told us that Max was shouting at Geoffrey about not being blackmailed?"

Another nod."

"Was he accusing Geoffrey?"

"I thought so at the time but now that I think of it, Geoffrey's reaction wasn't anger. It's almost as if Max was giving him an order. I think Geoffrey was agreeing."

Octavius unleashed one of his trademark "Hmmms"

The Captain came on the PA. "Folks, we'll be returning to Cairns tonight and ending our cruise midday. A ten hour run. Most of the time we hope you'll be pleasantly asleep. But we have a very special dinner planned for your last night with us. Gaston has outdone

119

himself and Lucinda will make sure your liquid requirements have been met."

"Oh, by the way, we have found a replacement for Ethan. Another dingo! His brother, Andy is also a graduate of the Australian Mixologist Institute. He's coming up from Brisbane to join our crew. He's unmarried. Lieutenant Cameron and I will be down to join you in the dining room and then we'll begin our journey north. Don't bother dressing up. We'll make it a casual celebration."

The prospect of drinks and snacks had inspired the Twins to return to the yacht. Tilda and the Tigers were sunning themselves. Belinda approached Bruce and Octavius.

"Plans for tomorrow. Depending on when we arrive back at Cairns, I'll have the Tigers check out the Aquabear and get it ready for our flight home. Mostly over water. We can fly supersonic. One stop. Honolulu and then on to Cincinnati. We may want to stay overnight in Cairns before starting the journey. I've asked Lucinda to book us into a good hotel close to the airport. I assume you and Tilda will fly commercial back to Melbourne."

"Sounds like a good plan, Belinda. It will give us a chance to talk firsthand to Ethan. I think he can give us more insight into what really happened to Geoffrey. Now that he's settled in Cairns with his mate, the pups and his new job, his memory of the incident may be sharper. What do you think, Ocko."

"Let's get him to meet us at the dock. See if you get Inspector McKenzie, too. How soon is dinner?"

*****

As the Reef Roamer sped northward, the Captain and First Officer had joined the merry band seated in the tastefully decorated dining salon. Chief Morgan was up at the bridge. A dinner tray was sent up to him. Jumbuck Chef Gaston was in his glory, periodically emerging from his kitchen to chat with the group and reap their praises over each delicious course. Lucinda was busy with the wines and non-alcoholics for the Twins. Ms. Baker was acting as Maîtress D' directing Alec and Henry who were doing waitstaff duty. This last-night dinner was an oft-repeated and carefully prepared event and carried off with superyacht precision.

Belinda and Octavius made speeches congratulating the crew, the boat and the tour company for a delightful week. Their comments were seconded by the Tigers, Tilda and Bruce. No mention was made of Geoffrey's demise and only one snide reference to the Minks came from the Twins. They were 'shooshed' by their mother.

The Captain felt no restraint, however. "Have you three detectives and the shoreside Inspector come up with a decision on Geoffrey Mink's death? I have to make a full report to the company and soon. Was it murder?"

Bruce replied, "We have strong suspicions and are following up double quick. It was no accident. He was struck too hard on the back of his head and his neck was broken. Even in that storm. a simple drunken fall at the jacuzzi steps wouldn't have produced those wounds. No, someone did him in. We're on it, It's a fair go we'll have our villain to rights by the end of day tomorrow. As far as I'm concerned, you and your crew are in the clear and that includes Ethan."

"Well, that only leaves the Minks."

"No comment!"

The Twins were about to add their opinion but were once more silenced by Belinda. Rolling of teen age eyes.

The First Officer and Lucinda rolled in a portable table stacked with oversize billed caps with Reef Roamer and the vessel's image embroidered on them. "A small souvenir of your tour. We had ones specially made to fit you two large Bears and Tigers. The ones with ear holes are for you Wallaroos."

The Twins grabbed two of the caps for themselves and then clapped one of the oversized versions on Octavius' head. "Yours should say, 'Champion Wake Boarder,' Dad. " Laughs!

Belinda took hers and rakishly set it over one ear. "Beats a Bearonial coronet any day!"

Bruce and Tilda got their long ears through the openings and admired each other. The Tigers said they would wear theirs while piloting the SST.

Nighttime on the Reef. Amazing! Not a cloud in the Southern sky. The Twins realized that they were seeing a different array of stars than they were used to at Polar Paradise. The Southern Cross, Alpha and Beta Centauri and the Jewel Box, all visible through the superyacht's telescope. No doubt, a powerful telescope was added to the juveniles' want list when they returned home.

They had already made a decision. Their next trip was going to be extraterrestrial. They'd have to persuade Howard and Marlin. They would probably get a big assist from their Mom who wanted to transit the universe. They weren't sure about Octavius. They could certainly get Otto who loved "zapping" around the galaxy. Maybe Maury, the Frau and Colonel. Who knows, maybe even Mlle Woof. Exoplanet Explorers! A new Internet game featuring The Bold Brave Brilliant Bumptious Bears was in the making. Little did their parents know what was in store for them.

Inside the salon, giggles, laughs, guffaws and more toasts as the evening progressed and the Reef Roamer got nearer to Cairns.

Chapter Twenty Four

In a conference room on the shore
They're reviewing the bidding once more.
Ethan starts his report
The Police cut him short.
The two Minks have escaped out the door.

Ten AM and the superyacht approached the dock. Inspector McKenzie was standing by as the vessel moved up to its berth. Evan was positioned away from the Inspector and stood by to tie up one of the hawsers. He cautiously looked over at the policeman. "I know. I don't work for them anymore. Force of habit."

The Grey Kangaroo grinned. "Don't worry, Dingo. You're off my suspect list. We just want to talk to you. Maybe scrape up a memory or two about that stormy night. Let's wait until Inspector Wallaroo, Tilda Roo and Doctor Bear can join us."

Evan grinned back. "That's good to know."

The Reef Roamer moored and Alec and Henry under Ms. Baker's direction started moving the passengers' luggage onto the dock and into the van. Goodbyes and hugs *(especially bear hugs)* all around.

Octavius asked the Captain if the detectives could use the conference room in the Tour Company's office for a short meeting. He checked and it was free. The next round of guests would be checking in in several hours. The Bear suggested the Twins and Benedict Tigris go to the snack bar at the foot of the quay and wait for the rest of the group to join them to make the trip to the airport hotel. Snacks were always welcome.

McKenzie, Tilda, Bruce, Belinda, Lucinda, Ethan, Galatea and Octavius entered the conference/waiting room and sat down or sprawled. The walls and every available surface were covered with pictures of the Great Barrier Reef. Distracting!

Octavius kicked the discussion off. "The subject is: Who Killed Geoffrey? Don't worry, Ethan. We don't think it was you but your memory of exactly what happened during that storm is crucial."

"I've been wracking my brains to remember the details ever since Inspector McKenzie called me. I think I have it straight."

"And you, Gal. You think Geoffrey was told by Max to deal with a blackmailer."

"Not in those exact word, Doctor Bear, but yes, I think so."

"OK, Ethan. If Bruce, Tilda and Inspector McKenzie agree, we're ready to hear your story."

Nods from the three detectives.

"Well, as I told you before, I was keeping the bar open as the storm approached in case anybody wanted a last minute drink. Dinner was a lost cause but a glass or two of Grog or a Dark N' Stormy might help with seasickness while getting pitched around. The Roamer was anchored rather than running with a drogue but was still going to feel the brunt of the winds, rain and waves."

"For a while, Geoffrey was my only customer. Minks have a pretty strong constitution for a small animal. Stronger than mine. But it was clear he was getting on. If he didn't get seasick, he was getting pretty drunk. Miranda came by, ignored him and asked for a shot of grog. Then she left."

"I thought Geoffrey was going back to his room when he attempted to stand on his four legs. Two of them slipped and he fell over. As I was about to come to his aid, the lights went out."

"A closet in the dining room had a supply of lanterns and flashlights and using the light app on my cell phone, I made my way there to pick up a supply for the guests. It was then I heard the storm doors in the salon slide open and the wind and rain poured in. I didn't realize Geoffrey had managed to get outside."

"I heard several animals coming into the bar. Miranda and Martha. Martha had picked up one of the large flashlights and was waving it around, turning it on and off. She went over to the open doors but was unable to close them. She went out to the jacuzzi. I went after her, afraid she'd be blown overboard. She screamed."

"The lights came back on. That's when I saw Geoffrey's dead body lying at the foot of the jacuzzi. His head and neck had taken several blows. Martha was having one of her hysterical fits. Miranda was standing by her, helping her stand. I noticed Martha no longer had the heavy flashlight but thought nothing of it. Now I wonder. Did she hit Geoffrey and then throw the flashlight overboard before the lights came on again. Anyway, I called the bridge. Cameron came down along with Alec. They called you. The rest you know."

Bruce asked, "Did you get a close look at this body. How did you know he was dead?"

"His head was twisted around and he was bleeding badly from his skull. I've seen fractured skulls and broken necks before. He was dead!"

"What did Martha and Miranda do."

"I told them to wait for an officer and one of you detectives but they ignored me and left. Then Ms. Baker came down and confirmed that he was dead."

Belinda asked, "So you think Martha might have clobbered him with the heavy flashlight and then tossed it overboard?"

"I think it's possible."

"Remember what Ursula told us about Martha?"

"Who's Ursula?" asked Ethan.

"A law enforcement associate of ours."

"She might have been blackmailing Max about money laundering to get him out of his job so she could run the company with her unidentified paramour."

Lucinda had been quiet throughout Ethan's recital but then spoke up. "Money laundering? Blackmail? You know, Martha had been using the ship to shore phone to call Manchester pretty frequently. I thought she was calling home but it may have been to Maximillian's offices. We keep a log. I can get it for you." She jumped up and left the room.

Octavius looked around the room. "Well, enforcers of the law. What do you think? Sufficient cause to detain the two of them? Personally, I find Martha very suspicious but you're the authorities."

McKenzie's cell phone rang. He nodded and frowned. "That was my office. Miranda and Martha just left on Japan Airlines for London with a stop in Tokyo. So much for flight risk. We should have confiscated their passports."

Bruce replied, "Well, that ties it for me. They think they can get on the safe side of an extradition order in England. I'll invoke my Interpol connections in Tokyo with the National Central Bureau of the National Police Agency to cut them off at the pass. Suspicion of murder, blackmail and money laundering should be enough to put them on an international hold and then get them back here. "

Belinda pondered what they were all thinking. "I wonder which one of them actually did it?"

Octavius broke the silence. "Let's gather up the Twins and Ben and head for the hotel. We have our own flights to take on tomorrow. Lucinda, once again, thank the crew and the company. All told, we've had a wonderful trip down under. Bruce and Tilda, Great to have been with you. Inspector McKenzie, good luck with the Minks. G'day all or is it Hooroo. mates?"

"Hooroo Ocko!

Epilogue

That's the end of the Cases Down Under.
The two Minks made a serious blunder.
Now a voyage through the air
To their friends at Bear's Lair.
So, what's next? Well you just have to wonder.

60,000 feet over the Pacific Ocean at Mach 2 heading toward Honolulu and ultimately, Cincinnati. Wonder of wonders, the Twins were sacked out and so was Octavius. The Tigers were at the controls and Belinda was sitting by herself in the oversize seats of the forward compartment of the Aquabear SST.

Contemplation time. They had spent the last three weeks and a lot of money in the world Down Under. On balance, it was delightful. She wouldn't have traded it for anything. The Twins were ecstatic and were coming home full of ideas for a new Internet game and requirements for water based equipment. Poor Harold. He was going to be swamped. *(No pun.)*

Octavius seemed to enjoy himself. I never expected to see him on a wakeboard but the big question remains. Did they accomplish what they set out to do? A slow transition into retirement.

During that same period, they had experienced two murders, contract rigging, money laundering, petty violence and several near misses – all involving Tavi. Was Bruce right when he said, "You're not really going to retire, are you? Leopards can't change their spots and bears can't shed their fur."

They needed to have another discussion. They also needed some input from the Octavians – Maury, Chita, Otto, the Frau and Colonel, Howard, Marlin, Condo and little Mlle Woof. Dougal and the Polar Paradise crew ought to be heard from as well. Maybe even those reprobates, Lion and Unicorn. Should they retire? Could they retire? Oh, well. Let's get back to Cincinnati.

Both legs – Cairns to Honolulu and Honolulu to Cincinnati passed without incident. In fact, they set a modest speed record over the Pacific. The Flying Tigers were jubilant and the Twins were busy incorporating the flight statistics into their new game: Bears Down Under.

At last, they made the same final approach to the Bear's Lair landing on the pseudo-Interstate that was really a runway for the Octavian Air Force. As they pulled up to the Roman Temple hangar, two crews descended on the aircraft. One started to unload the baggage and roll the airstairs up to the forward door out of which, as usual, the Twins shot and ran to the waiting welcoming committee.

(The second team was getting the tools and equipment ready to overhaul the Olympus engines, test the control surfaces and run full diagnostics on the instrumentation of the Concorde, Belinda's crown jewel. 'Keep 'em Flying!')

The Bold Brave Brilliant Bumptious Bears were hopping up and down, hugging the gathered Octavians and trying to tell everything about their adventures in thirty seconds flat. Octavius, Belinda, Ben and Gal walked down, made their appearances and stood by while the Twins dominated the event.

When they quieted down for moment, Frau Schuylkill made a short speech of welcome and suggested they enter the Bear's Lair where Huntley was standing by with champagne, mead and Scotch along with Fruit Smoothies and snacks, snacks and more snacks. The fur covered meteors needed no second invitation. Dinner would be coming soon but they could fill up in the meantime.

Maury approached. "G-day mates! Welcome back! Sounds like you had an exciting trip. Ursula has been keeping us up to date on your escapades and of course, we worked the bid rigging and money laundering activities on this end. Any news on the Mink Murder?"

The Great Bear rumbled. "Nothing dispositive but lots that's highly suggestive. The Australian police have it in hand."

Belinda smiled. "I'm glad they have it and we don't but I must admit my curiosity has been tweaked. I assume Bruce will keep us posted."

"Oh, no doubt. Or maybe Tilda. I wonder if those two are going to mate."

"I think they already have. They're just keeping it a secret."

Otto bounced up, a kelp juice cocktail in his paw. "Hey you guys. Are you waterlogged? I'm sorry I didn't come with you. That Great Barrier Reef sounds like an aquatic animal's paradise."

She replied "It is, Otto. We're sorry you didn't join us. But the Twins have talked us into stocking jetskis and kayaks at Polar Paradise. You and Harold can have a ball."

Otto looked at Octavius. "What? No wakeboards. Those pictures of you are hilarious."

The Great Bear took a swipe at him but as usual, he 'zapped' out of reach.

Condo begged off dinner. He needed to be back at the Hex for an important meeting. But first, he said how pleased he was with Ursula 13's performance. Octavius and Belinda agreed.

Howard had been listening to all this in silence. The porcupine grinned. " I don't suppose you two are up for another adventure right away. Decompression time. But Marlin and I have found a new exoplanet that we think is worth a look. Otto has given it a preliminary look-see. Sentient animals, breathable air, reasonable climate, no homo sapiens, reptiles or paranoid birds. Thought you and the Twins might be interested."

Belinda smiled. "Give us a couple of months. I have to return to Polar Paradise to keep up my bearonial status and resume my influence. But I said I wanted to do some quantum traveling and I meant it. I wonder if Tavi and I are adepts. We'll have to find out. I know the Twins are and so are you and Otto. Put it on the calendar."

*****

The utility chopper from Abeardeen Airport had just settled down in the Polar Paradise heliport. Dougal, Lord David and Mlle Woof were on hand to welcome the travelers. Chita was in London. Excited reunion between the Twins and their Bichon governess. Arabella produced a Reef Roamer cap for the little dog and she put it on at a jaunty angle. Laughs all around.

"Doctor Bear, we have a message for you from Australia. Inspector Wallaroo wants to talk with you. Somethin' about a murder."

Octavius looked at Belinda. "Let's see what he has to say. There's a nine hour difference so we'll have to wait until 10 PM Shetland time to reach them in their morning.."

At 10 PM, they placed a Zoom call to Bruce in Melbourne. Sure enough, Tilda was with him.

"Well, Ocko, the Mink Murder is wrapped up. As I think you know, we caught up with Miranda and Martha in Tokyo. Legal hoo-hahs and complications but McKenzie final brought them back to Cairns. More lawyers but we faced them down with evidence, circumstantial though it was. Long story short, Miranda broke down and accused Martha of killing Geoffrey with the heavy flashlight and then tossing it overboard in the storm. Martha denied it at first but finally admitted to bashing him. The Cairns authorities are holding Martha for murder and Miranda as an accessory."

"It seems Geoffrey was a busy boy. He was blackmailing Max about the money laundering, blackmailing Martha and her Manchester boyfriend on their attempts to take over the business. We still don't have an identification on Martha's paramour. Either a Director or Officer of the business. Neither Martha nor Miranda will give us his name. He might be tied into the money laundering but we're not sure."

"It looks like Geoffrey was putting too much pressure on them. He was threatening Miranda too. She was helping Martha with her takeover plans. All told, he was making enemies by the ton. The storm was too good an opportunity to pass up. He was drunk and they could fake his being swept away. They were ready to push his body overboard when the lights came back on and Ethan appeared. A quick change of story and Martha had another one of her phony cases of hysterics. Almost convinced us."

By the way, AUSTRAC and the UK National Economic Crime Centre (NECC); National Crime Agency (NCA) and the UK Financial Intelligence Unit are all throwing the book at Max. He's in deep doo-doo. I don't think he's going to bully his way out of this one."

"With the Minks all hung up, it's not clear who will take over the conglomerate if there's any conglomerate left to take over."

"Thought you'd want to know. Tilda says G'Day! By the way, Minister Cassowary has been completely exonerated both of bid rigging and the murder of Tasha Tasman. You've had an exciting visit to Oz. Hope you all enjoyed it. "

"That's for certain. Thanks, Bruce. This calls for a shot of mead."

Belinda laughed, "And champagne."

The End – Volume 16 – The Cases Down Under

About the Author

Harry DeMaio is a *nom de plume* of Harry B. DeMaio, successful author of several books on Information Security and Business Networks as well as the sixteen-volume *Casebooks of Octavius Bear.* He is also a published author for Belanger Books and the MX Sherlock Holmes series edited by David Marcum. A retired business executive, former consultant, information security specialist, elected official, private pilot, disk jockey and graduate school adjunct professor, he whiles away his time traveling and writing preposterous books, articles and stories.

He has appeared on many radio and TV shows and is an accomplished, frequent public speaker.

Former New York City natives, he and his extremely patient and helpful wife, Virginia, live in Cincinnati (and several other parallel universes.) They have two sons, living in Scottsdale, Arizona and Cortlandt Manor, New York, both of whom are quite successful and quite normal, thus putting the lie to the theory that insanity is hereditary.

His e-mail is hdemaio@zoomtown.com

You can also find him on Facebook.

His website is www.octaviusbearslair.com

His books are available on Amazon, Barnes and Noble, directly from MX Publishing and at other fine bookstores.

www.ingramcontent.com/pod-product-compliance
Lightning Source LLC
Chambersburg PA
CBHW080543180626
46818CB00008B/3114